P9-ART-761

IN HIS EYES

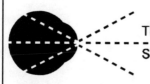

This Large Print Book carries the
Seal of Approval of N.A.V.H.

IN HIS EYES

GAIL GAYMER MARTIN

THORNDIKE PRESS

An imprint of Thomson Gale, a part of The Thomson Corporation

Detroit • New York • San Francisco • New Haven, Conn. • Waterville, Maine • London

LIBRARY OF CONGRESS CATALOGING-IN-PUBLICATION DATA

Martin, Gail Gaymer, 1937–
  In his eyes / by Gail Gaymer Martin.
    p. cm.
  ISBN-13: 978-0-7862-9315-5 (hardcover : alk. paper)
  ISBN-10: 0-7862-9315-2 (hardcover : alk. paper)
    1. Women architects — Michigan — Fiction. 2. Michigan — Fiction. 3. Large type books. I. Title.
  PS3613.A7786I54 2007
  813'.54—dc22
                                                 2006033399

Published in 2007 by arrangement with Harlequin Books S.A.

Printed in the United States of America on permanent paper
10 9 8 7 6 5 4 3 2 1

The eye is the lamp of the body.
If your eyes are good,
your whole body will be full of light.
— Matthew 6:22–23

This book is dedicated to my husband's aunt Florence and to Bob's wonderful Italian family.

They are filled with warmth, love and compassion.

Over the years, I've learned so much about his family's traditions and fun-loving spirit.

Thanks to my friend Marianne Funke who lived on Harsens Island and answered my questions.

Thanks to Esther from the Riverfront Shop who provided me with more information.

As always, I thank my husband for his hard work and support. He is a hero in my eyes.

CHAPTER ONE

"You want me to do what?"

Ellene Bordini's voice ricocheted around her office as she frowned at the telephone. She pursed her lips, waiting for her father's peevish voice to sail back at her.

Instead, she heard silence.

"I'm sorry, Dad, but —"

"Come in here, Ellene. We need to talk."

His quiet voice struck her harder than a slap. She'd tried his patience, and his response had been far more gentle than she'd deserved.

"All right," she said, humbled by his manner. She hung up the phone and clasped her hands together to calm her reaction to his request.

She knew better than to attack her father. She knew because she loved him and because the Bible said to honor her parents.

A prickle ran up her arms as she thought about her brother. Her position in the construction company should have been his — had he been alive. Her dad was proud of the family business, and her goal was to prove she could handle it with a firm hand.

Ellene ran her fingers through her hair, pulling out knots at the ends. She disliked her natural curl about as much as she disliked talking with Connor Faraday, but that seemed to be what her father expected.

Checking her calendar, she speculated when she'd have time to call Connor Faraday. Her father's insistence let her know she wouldn't change his mind, but she'd try. How could she talk business with the man who'd broken her heart? Grasping her fortitude, she rose and strode from her small office into the corridor, then crossed the hall to her father's office.

She lifted her hand and paused, gathering her thoughts, then rapped her knuckles against the solid wood door. For a woman of twenty-nine, she still felt a child's reaction to facing her father. When he invited her in, she drew a lengthy breath and turned the knob.

Syl Bordini sat behind his desk with his back to the door, a telephone receiver pressed against his ear. When Ellene stepped inside, he swivelled to face her, a grim look wrinkling his brow. "I'll have Ellene call you today to set an appointment. Thanks again for thinking of us."

Ellene stood close to the door, hoping his lecture for snarling at him would be quick and painless, but when he lowered the receiver, he motioned toward a chair, his look more tender than she expected. She closed the door behind her and settled across from him.

"I'm sorry, Dad, for —"

He waved his hand to brush away her words. "Ellene, this is our livelihood. Sometimes we must deal with people we'd rather not, but if they're honest and need our services, then we work with them. You wanted a position with the company, and I trusted that you could do the job."

He looked at her above his reading glasses, and she squirmed. "I can, Dad. Have I ever disappointed you?"

"Not at all. I'm pleased with your work. Very pleased."

A faraway look filled his eyes, and Ellene figured his thoughts had drifted to her brother who'd died in Bosnia.

His focus returned, and he shook his head. "Today I'm disappointed that you let the past influence your judgment. Business is business."

"I know business is business," she said.

"But this is different, Dad. It's Connor. We were engaged, and it ended badly. We have other employees who could do the job."

"He asked for you."

The words jarred her. Why? She searched for a logical reason, but none came.

Her father leaned closer, his voice softer. "He said he trusts your judgment."

But she didn't trust Connor's. She sat speechless, her mind sorting out her father's words.

"Listen, Ellene," he said, rising. His voice sounded like the father from her childhood. He walked around the desk and drew up a chair beside her. "I understand your feelings, but time has passed. Ten years."

"Not quite eight," she said. To her it still seemed like yesterday.

"Haven't you ever made a mistake?"

The night Connor left stuck in her memory like a tack, but today, a bittersweet sensation rolled across her thoughts. "I've made bad choices, Dad, but —"

"Sin is sin. Mistakes are mistakes. The Bible teaches us to forgive so that God will forgive us our mistakes. I don't know what you expected of Connor. You ended the engagement. You need to move on with your life. You're both adults now."

"Connor's married, Dad. I have moved on."

Her father took her hand and held it, his strong fingers covering hers. The warmth spread up her arm giving her a sense of safety, the same as when she had been a little girl. "He trusts you."

"If that's what you want, I'll handle it."

He gave her hand a firm squeeze. "I knew you would, Ellene. I think you've let this grudge go on too long. I know you've seen other fellows, but you've steered so far away from marriage or commitment, I'll die without grandkids and you'll die an old maid. I'd like to be a grandfather someday."

"I'm only twenty-nine."

"Going on forty." He gave her a wan smile, then rose and walked to his desk. "Here's his phone number." He extended a sheet of paper.

Ellene rose and took the memo, gazing at her father's familiar neat blueprint-style lettering. "I'll call him tomorrow."

"You'll call now. That was Connor on the phone when you walked in. I told him you'd call today."

Her stomach bottomed out.

"He's anxious to get the project under way."

"Where is the job?"

"On Harsens Island. It was his mother's place."

"Harsens Island? That's near Algonac."

He nodded. "When do we turn down a job, because it's a few miles away?"

Connor's face rose in her mind, his firm jaw, those crystal-blue eyes that melted her heart, his light brown hair that turned gold in the summer sun, the soft unruly waves she'd love to run her fingers through. Connor, the rat, who'd walked away with her heart and into the arms of another woman without looking back.

Her icy hand felt damp as she clasped the phone number. She looked into her father's eyes and gave up the battle. "I'll call Connor today, Dad."

Connor sat at a table along the restaurant wall, his eyes glued to the doorway. His knee wiggled beneath the tablecloth, and he tucked his hands in his lap to stop himself from playing with the silverware.

His nerves had never been so raw, at least not since years ago when his relationship with Ellene had ended. He'd asked himself over and over why he'd insisted that she work as the contractor with him. He knew Bordini Construction had a solid reputation. Any of their contractors would have

14

done an excellent job, but when he'd called the company, he'd done what his heart dictated.

He'd heard the tension in Ellene's tone when she'd called. Her voice had always raised the hairs on the back of his neck, the resonant tone filled with spirit and a light heart. Yesterday the lilt had seemed missing, replaced by a controlled voice that sounded so alien to him.

The waitress filled his coffee cup for the third time, and he pushed up his sleeve to check his watch again, wondering if she'd stood him up. Ellene had always had subtle ways to get even. She often joked about God's eye-for-an-eye philosophy, but most often, her true spirit had been to turn the other cheek.

Connor pulled his hand from beneath the table and lifted the cup as he observed the steam. Through the curling haze, he saw the restaurant door swing open, along with a chilly wind, and he held his breath.

Ellene.

At first glance, she hadn't changed except for the elegance of maturity. Her dark hair hung in loose curls to her shoulders, as he remembered. How many times had he run his fingers through the thick tendrils?

He lifted his hand, and when she saw him,

a tense look tightened her features. Her mouth set into a straight line, hiding the generous smile he recalled so easily.

She slipped off her peacoat, and he watched her cross the room, dressed in pants and jacket the color of blueberries. He didn't like blueberries, but he liked the deep-blue color against warm beige skin. The color illuminated her eyes.

"Hello," Connor said, rising. He longed to embrace her, but he sensed her apprehension and extended his hand.

She took it with a firm shake, then released his fingers and pulled out her own chair. "You look well," she said, her eyes focused everywhere but on his.

"So do you." He wanted to say so much more, but not today. She'd made it clear this was a business appointment. "Thanks for meeting with me."

"You're welcome. Dad sends his best wishes."

"We had a nice talk today." He admired Ellene's father. Though a shrewd businessman, he had always been honest and forthright.

She nodded, her eyes focused on the menu.

"I didn't know what to order you to drink," he said, lost for words. He had so much to say — things he longed to tell her, but he feared her response. Connor recoiled at the helpless feeling that washed over him.

"I'd like hot tea," she said, finally looking up. "I'm sorry I was late. I had to handle a call as I was leaving."

"No problem." Connor beckoned the waitress and ordered the tea, then perused the menu, hoping that time and silence might pull things into perspective. Nearly eight years had passed since he'd seen Ellene. Yet emotionally, he felt as if it had been the day before.

"It's been a long time," he said, unleashing the thoughts from his mind.

"Yes, it has."

She said nothing more, and he took his cue from her. He selected his meal, though his stomach had tied in knots from the moment he'd sat at the table.

The strained silence rattled him; he felt his knee bouncing beneath the table again, and he braced his heel against the floor, forcing his leg to steady. "I don't know if your dad told you, but I've inherited my mother's summer home on Harsens Island."

"I heard about your mom's death, Connor. I'm sorry."

"Thanks. She'd been ill for a while."

"I was very fond of your mom."

Warm memories filled him. "I know, and she was crazy about you." The silence in the air was charged with memories.

The waitress returned with the tea and took their orders. Ellene dropped the bag into the metal pot, then dipped it a few times. Finally she rolled the string around the bag, gave a pull and set it on the saucer.

Connor wanted to grab the pot and drain it into the cup to complete the ritual so they could talk. His leg began jigging again, and he stretched it out, determined to relax.

Ellene poured the tea, took a careful sip, then looked at him. "So, what can Bordini Construction do for you?"

Connor pulled his knee up sharply and whacked the bottom of the table. Her tea splashed over the edge into the saucer. "Sorry," he said, grabbing his napkin and dabbing the liquid.

"It's fine. That's what saucers are for."

He pulled away the soggy napkin and placed the dry side onto his lap, feeling like a gangling teenager. When he looked at Ellene, she gave him a wide-eyed gaze.

"Back to business," she said. "Dad said you wanted some work done. What kind of renovations are you talking about? What time frame are we discussing?"

"I'd like to enlarge both bedrooms, add a

garage. Possibly make the porch a year-round room."

"It's screened now."

He nodded, pleased that she remembered, because that might mean she recalled them together there, their kisses so emotional he had to rein in his longing, a yearning he controlled for her sake. He'd revered her upbringing and only wished he had continued that kind of restraint.

"We need another bathroom upstairs, too," he said as an afterthought.

Ellene's head jerked upward while an uneasy expression filled her face. "You said *we*. Now that I think of it, I'd feel more comfortable if your wife were with us, Connor. I'd like to hear her ideas in her own words."

Her question startled him. "Apparently you haven't heard."

Ellene's forehead wrinkled. "You're divorced?"

Her tone reminded him she didn't approve of divorce. "No. Melanie died. An aneurism. It all happened too fast. I wasn't prepared."

Ellene's frown faded. "I'm sorry, Connor. I hadn't heard." She lifted a finger and wound it through a strand of hair. "Sadly, falling in love offers no guarantees."

Her comment brought on difficult memories. "I know." His loving relationship with Ellene filled his mind with a rush of nostalgia. He gazed at the tilt of her head and the look in her eyes, unable to explain the rising sensation that fluttered through him like summer moths.

The twirled strand of hair fell into a ringlet when she lowered her hand. "So then who is the 'we' you mentioned?"

He pulled his gaze from the twist of hair. "My daughter. Caitlin. She's six."

Ellene's pulse skipped. "A daughter." Disbelief and sadness vied within her. She looked at Connor with fresh eyes. "A daughter," she repeated, picturing her career-filled life.

He shrugged as if not knowing how to respond. "It's been difficult raising her alone for the past couple of years."

"I'm sure it has," she said, trying to make sense of the sweep of emotion that overtook her. She could have married, too. She could've had a child and not just a career. The choice had been hers.

The waitress saved her from further conversation. Her salad arrived, and Connor's burger. They quieted, each delving into their meals. But Ellene's appetite had waned.

Connor, a dad. The vision filled her mind. As she swallowed, lettuce caught in her throat. She coughed, to no avail, then gave up and washed it down with a drink of tea.

Connor lowered his sandwich and wiped his mouth. "After mom died, the cottage seemed a perfect place to bring Caitlin. My mother's sister — remember my aunt Phyllis? — she lives next door, and we'll be close to her. It'll be good."

Ellene couldn't deal with all the details spilling from him. She pushed the greens around in her bowl, longing to get away and sort her emotions. She wanted to be distant and businesslike, but he'd dropped a surprise into the mix. A six-year-old daughter. A little girl without a mother.

Ellene remembered one of her friends losing her mother when they were both children. How did a child deal with the loss? How had Connor explained his wife's death? And without a strong faith, what hope had Connor offered his child?

She jerked her mind back to their business. "When do you want me to see the cabin?"

"What's good for you?"

Not this, she thought. Ellene felt Connor's knee jerking beneath the table. He always did that when he was edgy. She leaned down to pick up her handbag tucked beneath her chair. "I don't know," she said, unzipping the top and pulling out her daily planner.

She tilted the notebook away from Connor. Free days rose from the page, but her self-preservation fought going to the familiar cabin and seeing the little girl. Caitlin, he'd called her. A good old Irish name to go with Faraday. What might she and Connor have named their daughter? A knot twisted in her chest.

Ellene felt Connor's gaze on her, and she lifted her focus from the planner. Her heartbeat skipped when she saw the look in his crystal-blue eyes. She could never forget his eyes or the elfin grin that looked so mischievous it made her laugh.

Today she saw only confusion.

"How about next week? Thursday or Friday?" she asked.

A frown sprang to his face. "Is this Saturday bad for you?"

"Saturday?"

"Caitlin goes to elementary school during the week. I'd rather not take her out of classes."

She hadn't thought. "Saturday's fine, Connor. I'll be there in the early afternoon." And get it over with.

He nodded as she forced her attention back to her lunch. But who felt like eating?

CHAPTER TWO

Saturday, Ellene pulled into the Champion Auto Ferry parking lot and got in line with nothing to do but watch the ferry maneuver across Lake St. Clair from Harsens Island to the mainland. The wintry March sun struck the gray snow piled along the bank, but the feeble rays didn't penetrate the cold outside her car. Enormous ice floes jammed against each other and struck the nose of the boat as it moved to shore.

She rolled down her window to pay the five-dollar toll while a bitter wind swept inside her car and sent a chill down her back. The outer cold seemed no more icy than her internal struggle.

Today she'd face Connor again, but this time on his turf. Since she'd seen him earlier in the week, she'd wavered between nostalgia and bitterness. The good times rolled sweetly into her thoughts, but she tossed them out like old shoes, not wanting to deal with the hurtful memories.

Ellene focused ahead of her, past the sun's rays glinting off the hood of her car. Why couldn't she let the sunny memories of their relationship stay forefront in her mind? She squinted at the glare as the ramp dropped into place and the cars began to roll forward.

As the ferry boat propelled into the channel, she felt the jar of the ice floes and watched new snowflakes settle on her windshield. Summer seemed the time for island life, not the end of winter.

When they reached the other side, Ellene glanced at Connor's directions before leaving the ferry. It had been years since she'd been to the cabin, and Connor had always driven.

She veered the car down South Channel Road toward Middle Channel, passing a border of dried plume grass that grew tall along the banks. When she came to the party store, she knew she was close.

She slowed, her heart beating overtime. Questions barraged her. Why was she so nervous? Why couldn't she put the past behind her as her father had suggested? Why couldn't she accept the blame — or some of it — for their breakup? But she couldn't. She wanted nothing to do with Connor, child or no child.

Still, she had to admit, before she'd met him for lunch, she'd often thought about an older Connor. Would he look the same? Would he be bald or paunchy? Their meeting had answered her curiosity.

Connor had become a handsome man. Maturity had broadened his chest and toned his muscles so that his trim frame looked solid and healthy. His smile hadn't changed, and only the small crinkles around his eyes added something new to his character.

Her grip tightened on the steering wheel when she saw the log cabin. She pulled into the driveway, sending up a prayer that God would give her guidance and soften her attitude.

She sat a moment, thinking of her feelings — pride, hurt, dismay. Connor had wounded her and left her disillusioned. But she'd rebounded, dating one man, then another, never feeling drawn to any of them, but longing to get even with Connor for his rejection.

Connor's rejection had been the first, but not the last. Only last year she'd thought she had found another man who'd expressed his love and devotion. A few months ago, she'd learned he'd cheated on her. Her skin crawled with the memory.

That day, Ellene had realized that few men could be trusted. She didn't need a man. Today she was determined to work for her father and make him proud.

As she headed up the driveway, the side door opened. Connor peeked out and grinned. "Cold, isn't it?" His brown-and-white checkered shirt beneath a deeper brown sweater gave him a homey charm.

She couldn't help but grin back at his stupid question. "You could have waited until May for this."

"Not really. I want to get settled here during the summer when Caitlin is out of school."

Caitlin. The name whacked her in the chest. As she stepped inside, she gave the room a quick scan, expecting the child to be there. But she wasn't in sight, and the fact aroused Ellene's curiosity.

She covered her discomfort by surveying the open space of the great room, dining and kitchen all in one. "I'd forgotten how nice this is," she said, admiring the expansive room. "You have lots of space to work with. I like it."

"I like it, too, but it's the —"

"I hate it here!"

The child's shout pierced their subdued conversation, followed by the sound of a crash above their heads as if she'd thrown something across the room.

"Sorry," Connor said. "She's having one of her bad days."

"You never let me do anything," Caitlin bellowed down the staircase.

Ellene flinched at the child's frustration.

Connor walked to the narrow opening and called up the stairs. "Caitlin, stop it. We have company."

"I don't care. I don't want any company."

"She doesn't mean it," he said, looking at Ellene with contrition in his eyes. He turned and bolted up the stairs, and Ellene waited, listening to the commotion from above.

Finally it quieted, except for a child's sobs. Ellene's heart wrenched at the sound.

Connor's footsteps thudded down the stairs and paused at the bottom. "Sorry. This is too common lately."

Ellene felt at a loss. "What do you do?"

"Let her cry it out. I don't know what else to do. To be honest, once in a while I'd like to give her a good spanking, but that's not what she needs."

His comment sparked her curiosity. "What does she need?"

"A mother to give her more attention than I can."

Ellene felt a shudder course through her, and she clasped her handbag tighter to her body. The sorrow she felt for Connor at that moment overwhelmed her. "It must be hard for you." She tilted her head toward the staircase. "What do you do when she acts out this way?"

"She's in time-out with threats of no TV."

"No TV? I suppose that's a good punishment."

He nodded. "Caitlin's shy and hasn't made friends around here yet. TV's her major form of entertainment."

As he stepped forward, a disconcerted look registered on his face. "I really apologize for all this." He extended his hand. "I didn't even take your coat."

Ellene slipped it from her shoulders and handed it to him.

"Have a seat. I'll make some coffee."

"You don't need to do that," she said, rattled by the child's problems and her own sensations.

Ellene's emotions flew to opposite poles — pity and envy. If she and Connor had married, they might have had a daughter. Then she would be a mother, not knowing what to do either with an unhappy child.

While Connor strode into the kitchen area, Ellene settled into a chair and gazed through the glass door to the large porch and the channel beyond, weighing her thoughts and calming her discomfort while Conner put on a pot of coffee. When he finished he headed across the room to Ellene.

"I want to make things better for Caitlin," he said, sinking into the chair across from her. "She'll make friends eventually, once she starts school here. Aunt Phyllis will be good for her. Caitlin needs a woman in her life, and even though . . ."

Connor's voice melded into Ellene's muddied thoughts. Caitlin needed a woman — but, as Connor had just said, the girl needed a mother. Every child deserved to be loved and nourished by a motherfigure. Ellene recalled Connor's elderly aunt. She had been a nice woman, but would she be able to deal with the energy and needs of a young, lonely child?

"I shouldn't be yakking so much," Connor said, his voice impinging into her reverie. "You don't want to hear my problems."

Ellene hadn't heard them, except she understood his frustration. "I feel for you,

Connor. Being a parent is a big responsibility."

"And being a single parent is even bigger."

Ellene nodded, not knowing what else to say. They gazed at each other until she became uneasy. "I suppose we should get down to business."

"Right. The business." The scent of coffee filled the air, and Connor rose again, pulled down three mugs from the cabinet and grabbed a packet from a nearby box.

Hot chocolate for Caitlin, Ellene guessed. *Connor has a soft heart.* The awareness pressed against her chest.

Connor poured the coffee and handed Ellene a cup, then strode to the staircase. "Caitlin, if you can be a good girl, you can come down for some cocoa."

He stood a moment listening, then shrugged. But in a moment, footsteps sounded on the steps, and Ellene's gaze shifted back to the staircase opening. In a heartbeat, a spindly child, dressed in pink sweatpants and shirt paused in the doorway. Her eyes were red-rimmed, and an occasional hiccup let Ellene know she was controlling her sobs.

When she inched into the room, she headed straight for Connor who was putting a mug into the microwave. She reached him and buried her face into his pant leg, wrapping her arms around his leg.

"Can you say hello to Ellene?" Connor asked, resting his hand on the child's dark-blond hair.

She didn't raise her head but curled even closer to Conner and gave a shake.

Connor crouched and tilted her eyes to his, whispering something Ellene couldn't hear. When he rose again, Caitlin stood straighter, watching the microwave above her head. Hearing the quiet beep, Connor pulled out the mug, added the chocolate mixture and stirred, then set it on the counter. "Let it cool a minute or you'll burn your hands."

He grasped his mug of coffee and headed for Ellene. "I suppose you don't approve." He passed the chair and sat on the couch.

She frowned, wondering what he meant.

He gave a slight tilt of his head toward Caitlin. "Forgiving too quickly."

Forgiving too quickly. The words shot through her as her father's words pierced her thoughts. *The Bible teaches us to forgive so that God will forgive us our mistakes.* "I don't think you were wrong."

He gave her a questioning look, as if he wasn't sure if she meant it, then turned toward Caitlin. She'd grasped the mug of chocolate and was blowing on the top. Connor patted the cushion beside him.

Caitlin noticed, but hesitated.

"Hi, Caitlin. I'm glad to meet you," Ellene said, watching the child's unsteady journey with her hot drink.

Caitlin gave her a shy look, then moved closer and finally settled beside Connor.

Ellene took a sip of the coffee, surprised that Connor remembered she liked it with milk, and studied the child. She saw Connor's image in the little girl, and it was more than the blue eyes. Caitlin had the same determined set to the jaw. What looked different was her nose, more delicate and slightly rounded at the tip. The early thought rose in her mind. What would her and Connor's little daughter have looked like? If . . .

No ifs. She clinched her jaw, struggling to gain control of her thoughts and let her question slide. She focused on Caitlin, wishing she could do something to bring a smile to the child's face, something to help her relax. "Do you know why I'm here?"

Caitlin shook her head as she glanced toward her dad.

"I'm here to fix your new house for you."

"I don't want a new house," she mumbled.

Her response startled Ellene. She figured

most kids would love the excitement of moving to a new house. "You don't think it'll be fun to have new adventures and make new friends?"

The child looked away, never letting her gaze land on Ellene. "I don't want new friends. I hate it here."

Ellene flinched again at the child's vehemence. "Why?"

The simple question seemed to stump the girl. She looked down at the floor, then into her cocoa mug and shrugged.

"I'd love to live on an island," Ellene said, knowing that she'd stretched the truth a bit. She'd enjoy the island in the summer.

Caitlin gave her a wary look, but for the first time, had finally looked into her eyes.

Ellene's chest tightened at the visual contact. "Your daddy —" The word hurt to say. "— can take you in a boat in the summer, and you can go swimming on the beach. And in the wintertime, you can —" Can what? Freeze to death was all she could think of.

"Tell Ellene what we're going to do with your bedroom," Connor said, filling Ellene's abrupt silence.

Caitlin shook her head. "I don't want a new bedroom."

Hearing the child's plaintive voice, Ellene

felt rocked with compassion and set her cup on the table. She and Connor needed to get to their business, but Caitlin's unhappiness engulfed her.

Ellene's mind spun with actions. Not confident in her tack, she rose. "Why don't you show me your room? Maybe you could tell me what another girl might like if she lived in this house. I bet you have good ideas."

The child studied her a minute, and to Ellene's amazement, she stood, eyed her dad and then headed toward the stairway. Ellene gave Connor a sidelong look and followed.

Connor watched them head up the stairs, then stood to follow but changed his mind. He'd leave well enough alone. Maybe Caitlin would soften her belligerence, and Ellene would see the sweet child she really was.

He drained his cup, set it on the table and wandered to the glass doorway that led to the porch. Outside he saw the crystallized snow that rimmed the lake. His gaze drifted to the porch love seat while memories swept him away.

He and Ellene had visited the cottage more than once, and they'd sat on the porch, occasionally alone, where he could sneak a kiss. He recalled her soft lips. They were young and inexperienced, not that he'd wanted to be. He'd listened to the guys in the high school locker room relate their conquests, brag about their prowess, and he'd laugh and nod as if he knew what they were talking about.

But he'd respected Ellene too much even to suggest anything like that to her. Now that he thought back, he wondered where he'd gotten such self-control. He'd wanted to know the secrets that his buddies bragged about, but his morals had stopped him from tempting fate.

So why in college had he succumbed so easily to Melanie? He'd been hurt by Ellene's rejection. Rejection? The excuse sounded so weak. They'd promised to marry after he graduated from college — only a couple of years to wait. Ellene had been the only woman he'd really loved.

Rejection was no excuse for his behavior. He'd gotten involved with Melanie on the rebound. She'd been attractive and more romantically experienced, and he'd thought . . .

Connor listened to the sounds above him, longing for life to have taken a different turn. Would his life have been different if he'd controlled himself with Melanie? Could he have resolved the problem with Ellene and gotten back together?

Though he'd tried, Connor couldn't remember how he and Ellene had become friends, but they had. They had been raised differently. She'd been born into a family he'd never experienced. Her parents lived well, enjoying their Italian heritage. He could picture the lovely home surrounded by flowers and trees. Her mother, always neatly dressed, wore jewelry and perfume. She attended social functions and volunteered at one of the charity foundations, while her father ran the family business. They had money and luxuries. Their family gatherings were loud and full of food and love.

His own family struggled to make ends meet. His mom worked behind the counter at a dollar store, and his dad worked in a small factory, coming home with grime beneath his fingernails and smelling of cigarette smoke.

Another noise from above caused Connor to turn and look up. Enough of wondering what was happening with Caitlin and Ellene. He strode across the room and up the staircase.

The second story reminded him why Ellene had come to the cabin. The upper floor held two small rooms with limited closet space, hardly a place for a young girl to feel at home. Caitlin had the larger room, but the smaller one had become a storage area with boxes and unused furniture that needed to be tossed out. Connor longed to make one lovely room for Caitlin with space to spare.

He strode past the smaller room and stood outside Caitlin's door. "So how's it going?" he asked as he stepped inside.

Ellene was sitting on the corner of the bed while Caitlin stood in the middle of the room, pointing toward the closet.

"Are you telling Ellene what you want up here?"

"I don't want anything. I told you." Her piercing voice was followed by the sweep of her hand across a night table. The contents clattered to the floor. "You never listen to me. I'm telling her what the other girl wants."

"What other girl?" he asked.

The child's face darkened to crimson as she shook her finger at him. "The girl Ellene said who'll live in this house."

"That's enough, Caitlin." Connor struggled to keep his voice calm. He stepped forward, catching her by the arm and drawing her to his side. "I'm sorry. I forgot, but you can't be rude like this."

Ellene rose from the bed and edged toward the door, looking uneasy. "I'll be downstairs."

He returned his attention to Caitlin, embarrassed that Ellene had to see his daughter's worst behavior. He closed his eyes a minute to gather his thoughts. "I can't let you treat an adult this way, Caitlin. If I were mean to you then I might deserve this, but I love you, and I only want the best for you."

Her belligerent look faded as tears pooled in her eyes and she reached up for him to lift her into his arms. She tilted her head forward and rested her chin on his shoulder, tears flowing onto his shirt. His chest heaved with sadness as he cuddled his daughter. Lately she'd changed from a shy, quiet child to a withdrawn, angry one.

Connor held Caitlin in his arms, smelling the lemony scent of her shampoo mingled with the chocolate aroma on her breath. After she quieted he settled her on the bed and stood beside her, caressing her hair while his vision blurred from the moisture in his own eyes.

What could he do? He wanted to invest in a new business — his own business — and he couldn't do that without more financing. His house in the Detroit suburbs would bring a good price and help start his business and still pay for renovations on the cottage. He'd do anything to make Caitlin content, but he didn't think the house or cabin had anything to do with it. Caitlin needed attention. She needed love, and he couldn't seem to give her enough of either.

"I want you to stay here until you feel like being more friendly. Ellene is here on business, and I have to talk with her."

Caitlin didn't respond. He shook his head and turned to the stairs.

"What kind of business?"

Her soft voice surprised him, and he turned toward her. "She's a building contractor."

"What's that?" She rolled over to face him.

Connor's chest tightened seeing her confused face. "She's a person who helps remodel a business or a house. She helps people decide which rooms to add or how to change them."

Caitlin frowned. "But she seems like your friend."

"I've known her and her father for many years."

"She has a daddy, too?"

"Yes. Mr. Bordini."

"And a mommy?"

A lump caught in Connor's throat. "Yes."

"I thought so."

Fighting a lump in his throat, Connor could only nod.

Caitlin rolled back to face the wall.

"I'll talk to you later, sweetheart," he said, heading once again for the staircase.

"I know. You got business," she mumbled.

Business. Yes, he had business with Ellene, but the word seemed so incompatible with the deeper relationship they'd once had. Seeing her now brought back those old unpleasant feelings. No surprise, really. Their parting had been shocking to him. He wondered if she'd ever realized how devastated he'd been. It hadn't been what he'd wanted, but pride and stubbornness had stopped him from begging her to take back the ring. He'd walked away.

Things happen for a reason, and later he'd realized the breakup had probably been for the best. Since Connor hadn't been a strong Christian then, he'd feared he could never meet her parents' expectations or make Ellene happy. Their relationship, he worried, would have brought heartache for everyone.

At the bottom of the stairs, Connor drew in a lengthy breath, then stepped into the room.

Ellene stood by the doorway, looking through the window into the porch.

"Today isn't a good day for Caitlin."

When he spoke, she turned to face him. "It's probably because I'm here." She lifted a finger and drew it around a lock of hair.

"It's not that." He wanted to explain, but he didn't have the answer himself. It was so many things.

She seemed to wait, and when he didn't add to his comment, she glanced at her watch. "It's getting late. I should finish up here and get on my way."

His pulse skipped as she stepped closer to him. "By the time we finish, it'll be getting dark. How about staying for dinner?"

She hesitated, then stiffened. "No, Connor, but thanks. Let's get started. I would really like to finish before dark. It's a long drive home."

Connor feared he'd pushed too hard, and he knew Ellene too well. When she meant business, that was it.

A sarcastic tone edged his words. "Okay, let's get this finished."

CHAPTER THREE

After an hour of talking about the cabin, Ellene settled onto one of Connor's dining-
room chairs and lifted the lid on her laptop.
She opened her software program and
began pulling together the renovation details
they'd discussed.

Connor had finally left her alone while he
worked at the kitchen counter, probably
preparing their evening meal. She glanced
at him occasionally, seeing him stare into
the refrigerator and study the inside of the
pantry. She forced herself to concentrate.
She needed to input the figures and ideas
they'd discussed, then get on the road. The
trip home would take over an hour even
without the weekday traffic, and the longer
she stayed the more confused she became.
For so many years, she'd dragged around
her negative attitude about Connor, yet
today he'd even made her laugh.

She studied the yellow legal pad as a

garbled notation hopped from the page. "You're willing to lose four feet of the great room to expand the bathroom and bedroom downstairs. Is that what we agreed? I can't read my notes."

"Right. If we make the porch a year-round room, I can spread the sitting area out even more, and we'll leave the far end of the porch as it is." He glanced her way. "Is that right?"

"The last twelve feet will remain a screened-in porch. Correct." Her fingers flew across the keyboard, and she only noticed Caitlin when her shadow fell over her scribbled notes.

The girl leaned over her shoulder and looked at the screen. "What are you doing?"

"I'm typing information."

"Can I type?"

"I'm working right now, Caitlin, but I know computers are fun. They have all kinds of information and even programs for kids."

Caitlin drew back. "I know."

Ellene chuckled at her blunt retort.

The little girl touched the edge of the keyboard. "We have computers at my school."

"Computers are the backbone of com-munication."

Caitlin's face screwed into a disbelieving look. "Computers don't have backbone. People do."

Ellene laughed and glanced at Connor who sent her a wry smile. "I mean, it's very important in business. We can talk with people all over the world."

Caitlin lifted her eyebrows. "Talk?"

"Not talk, but write to people or read information from other countries."

"On e-mail," Caitlin said.

The child's simple response made Ellene grimace at her lack of experience talking with children.

Caitlin faced Connor. "Daddy, we should get a computer for home, too."

He arched an eyebrow. "Maybe we should, but Caitlin, right now, you shouldn't bother Ellene."

"It's okay," But was it? Ellene felt her heartstrings tangling around the little girl. She needed to remain uninvolved before she got hurt again.

Caitlin leaned closer to the monitor. "Do you have games on your computer?"

"A few." Ellene paused a moment to shoo her away, then thought better of it and hit the minimize button. "This is the desktop. See this right here." She cringed suspecting Caitlin knew about the desktop.

Caitlin nodded as Ellene clicked an icon. A noise hummed and clicked as a machine came onto the screen while Caitlin giggled.

"What's that?" the child asked, pressing her finger against the monitor.

"It's pinball. You're too young for this game, but adults like it."

Caitlin leaned closer, watching Ellene shoot the ball. "We don't have games like that at school."

The sound pulled Connor from the kitchen area, and he wandered to her side and leaned over, viewing the screen. "I've never played computer games."

"You're kidding," Ellene said. "What world do you live in?" Silence hung between them for a moment.

"The world of a single dad."

Her stomach knotted, getting his message.

"Look," she said, hoping to ease the uncomfortable moment. "Here are the keys to use the flippers and bumpers, and you use the space bar to shoot the ball."

Caitlin giggled as Ellene's ball skittered across the screen, bouncing into a worm hole and rattling against the bumpers. She gave the ball another whack, and it rebounded, sending her score upward.

"My turn!" Connor said, then chuckled at himself. "Could I try?"

She grinned at the childlike way he'd requested a chance to play, and she rose, allowing him to slip into the chair. He tested the keys, getting used to the flippers, before he began his turn. When he shot the first ball, he missed, and it vanished down the chute. No score.

He gave her a silly grin while his knee tapped as he pushed the space key that triggered the ball into the playing field.

Ellene forgot herself, watching him play the game and delighting in Caitlin's amazement. But, noticing the clock hands, she realized too much time had slipped away. She'd let down her guard and had gotten caught up in Connor's company. That wasn't supposed to happen.

She touched Connor's shoulder, aware of the muscles that rolled beneath her palm. "I need to get going, Connor. I have to break up your fun."

He halted and dropped his hand from the keyboard. "Sorry. I got carried away."

Caitlin slipped her arm around his shoulder. "Get us one, daddy," she pleaded in his ear. "We can play games."

"It keeps them busy," Ellene said, seeing the excitement on Caitlin's face.

Caitlin pressed her palms on Connor's cheeks and turned his face to hers. "It keeps

47

kids busy, Daddy."

Ellene hid her grin.

Connor rose, and Ellene slipped back into the chair without comment.

Caitlin continued to watch her as she input the data. Ellene longed to get out of there and finish the job back in the office, but she feared she couldn't read what she'd scribbled.

The aroma of ground meat drifted around her, and her stomach gnawed silently. She wished he'd let her leave before preparing their meal, but glancing at the time, she realized he had every right to get their dinner ready.

One notation confused her, and she stopped and reread the note. "Connor, we need to double-check the porch." She rose and headed for the doorway.

When she looked back, Connor had lowered the burner on the stove and turned to follow her. They stepped into the icy surroundings. Snowmobiles flew across the frozen channel, drawing her memory back to the large hunks of ice jamming against each other in the water as she crossed Lake St. Clair from the mainland.

She shivered, and Connor drew nearer, his arms rising, then lowering again as if he wanted to put them around her. "It's too cold to be out here without a coat," he said.

"It'll only take a minute." She hurried to the far side of the enclosure and pointed. "We want to begin the screened porch here."

"Right."

She handed him the end of the tape measure and backed up to the far wall. "Sixteen feet for the room's length, then. I know it's eleven and a half wide." She drew in the tape as she returned to him. "What about this window over the sink? What did you decide?"

"You suggested leaving it as a window to pass food out for a picnic, and then you said you could block it with shelving on the inside." He rubbed his temple as if the action would clear his memory. "I think that was it."

"Which do you prefer? I like the opening."

"Me, too, but what I'd really like is to get you inside." He stepped behind her and grasped her arms, then shifted her around to face the doorway into the house. The heat from his nearness swept up her arms into her chest, and she felt his warm breath against her cheek.

Ellene longed to jerk from his grasp, but the feeling was too pleasant. Fighting her own longing, she eased away with her one-word reminder. "Business."

Connor's gaze lowered, and his smile faded. "It's easy to forget."

"Well, don't, or you'll have to find another contractor to handle this." She winced. Once again, she could see her father's face as he reprimanded her for not letting the past go and not handling the job like a professional.

Connor pushed open the outside door, and when they stepped in, Caitlin was sitting in the chair, staring at the computer.

Connor sucked in a gasp. "You didn't touch anything, did you sweetheart?"

The child looked at him with a frown. "No."

"Good," he said, ignoring the look. He moved toward the fireplace and tossed a log onto the kindling, then struck a match.

Ellene watched mesmerized as the kindling burst into flames and licked upward toward the bark. The flicker lent a homey look to the large room.

When she turned, Caitlin scooted off the chair and let Ellene sit again to finish her work. She glanced at her watch. "I'm just about done." She scrolled the document, then hit Save and closed the program.

The aroma from Connor's dinner preparations blanketed her. This time her stomach gave a soft growl.

Caitlin tittered at the sound, then stepped back to let Ellene rise. "Are you going home?"

"I sure am. It's late."

Connor looked over his shoulder. "Why won't you eat with us, Ellene? It's almost ready. Goulash. Not gourmet but filling."

"Eat with us," Caitlin said, a whole different child than Ellene had met when she arrived.

"Sorry. I really must go."

She closed the computer and snapped the lock, but as she reached for the handle, the side doorbell chimed. Before Connor answered it, the door swung open. An elderly woman in a navy pea jacket slipped inside, wearing boots that looked big enough to fit Connor. When she turned, Ellene recognized Connor's aunt.

"Aunt Phyllis," Connor said, stepping over to give her a hug. "Come in. You remember Ellene."

The woman's eyes widened in surprise. "The mind isn't what it used to be, but I could never forget Ellene." She grasped Ellene's hand and gave it a squeeze. "How are you dear? It's so good to see you."

"I'm fine, and nice to see you," Ellene

51

said, surprised at the woman's warm greeting.

Aunt Phyllis dragged snow across the room as she sought Caitlin and pulled her into an embrace.

"You're too cold," Caitlin said drawing back.

"It's colder than the Arctic out there, and it's starting to snow heavily again."

Connor shifted to the fireplace, tossing on a smaller branch, then poked at the wood, sending sparks skittering up the flue.

Snow. Ellene had seen enough snow the past year to keep her happy for many white Christmases. "Then I'd better —"

"Did you just drop by for a visit?" Connor's aunt asked.

"Not really. My father owns Bordini Construction, and I'm working up an estimate for a renovation project."

Connor gave her a disappointed look, and Ellene realized he hadn't shared the information with his aunt.

"Sorry," she mouthed, trying to block the view from Aunt Phyllis. "He's just thinking about it," Ellene added, hoping to smooth her faux pas.

"I wanted to surprise you, Aunt Phyllis, once I knew it was a go. I know how disappointed you get when —"

"God be praised," the woman said. "I'd have my prayers answered if you were thinking of moving here, Connor. I don't like being alone on the island when things happen."

When things happen. The words sounded ominous, but Ellene wasn't going to ask what things. Not knowing seemed the lesser of evils.

Aunt Phyllis pulled off her jacket and lapped it over the back of a chair. "Last year we were without electricity for nearly a week when the lines froze. It's not uncommon here on the island."

Connor sputtered a laugh. "Aunt Phyllis if you're trying to encourage me to move to the island, that won't help my enthusiasm."

"Let the Lord be in charge, Connor."

Ellene felt her brows lift, wondering what she meant.

Aunt Phyllis must have noticed her arched eyebrows and Connor's gaping mouth. "Proverbs sixteen," she said. "A man plans his course, but the Lord determines his steps."

Ellene hid her grin as she watched Connor sort through the words. Her gaze shifted to the blaze dancing in the fireplace while glowing embers sprinkled from the grate onto the hearth.

"You can plan all you want, Connor," his aunt said, "but if the good Lord wants you living on the island, that's where you'll be."

Connor scooted past her and whispered in Ellene's ear as he headed for the stove. "If the good Lord or Aunt Phyllis wants it. That's why I was keeping mum . . . until I was positive."

"Sorry," Ellene said. But she couldn't help but grin, hearing the woman putting Connor in his place. "I suppose I'd better —"

"Something smells good." Phyllis turned toward the stove and leaned around Connor's back to look into the pan. "Goulash. I haven't had that in a long time."

"You're welcome to join us."

"I wouldn't be in the way?" She looked at Ellene as if asking her.

"You're not in the way," Connor said. "You're always welcome to eat with us when we're here."

"I wasn't worried about you," Phyllis said. "I was asking Ellene."

Ellene pressed her hand against her chest. "Me?"

Phyllis nodded. "You're the guest here."

"But I'm leaving. I was just getting my things together."

Phyllis tilted her head to the side, a wry

look on her face. "Leaving?"

"I'm heading home," Ellene said again.

Phyllis broke into a chuckle. "You're not going anywhere."

"I'm not?"

"That's what I came over to tell you. The ice is jammed tighter than a jar of pickles. You're not getting off this island tonight. Maybe not even tomorrow from what I hear."

CHAPTER FOUR

Connor watched Ellene's expression droop. "It happens in winter, Ellene."

"It happens? You mean you live here with all these unexpected events — no ferry service, no electricity, no . . . I can't imagine wanting —"

"It's an adventure," Connor said, trying to stop her before Caitlin joined in the cry of not wanting to live on the island, either.

"You call this an adventure?" Ellene asked.

Connor drew Caitlin closer to his side. "We like adventures, don't we? We've had times we just climbed into the car and drove off. No destination. Just looking for adventure. Then we'd end up —"

"At the cider mill," Caitlin said, "and one time the fair. I like surprises."

Ellene's eyelids lowered as if she realized what she'd almost done. "Surprises are fun," she said, as if finally understanding Connor's concern. "But I really need to get home. That's not the surprise I was hoping for. Isn't there something they do to keep the ice from freezing at the ferry landing?"

Connor realized she was trying to sound upbeat, but he saw the look in her eyes. "Of course, they try, but nature is nature."

"They must do something?"

Aunt Phyllis chuckled. "The coast guard brings in the *Bramble* to see what she can do."

"Coast guard?" Ellene gave a fleeting look toward Connor, then turned her attention to Aunt Phyllis. "What's the *Bramble?*"

"The coast guard cutter," Connor said.

She looked befuddled. "Are you kidding?"

"No. The *Bramble* breaks up the ice, but once the thaw begins they have a big job keeping the ice from packing against the shoreline. The ice jam not only halts the ferry service, but it stops the freighters' access through the channel into the lake."

"They can't expect people to be stranded here forever."

Aunt Phyllis moved closer and patted Ellene's shoulder. "Not forever, dear. Only heaven is forever. It lasts a few hours or a few days." She gave Ellene's shoulder another pat. "Sometimes two or three weeks at the most."

Ellene's eyes widened. "You're kidding."

"No, she's not," Connor said. "If it lasts too long, the coast guard flies in emergency helicopters to give those in need access to the mainland for food or illness. We couldn't live on the island without the coast guard."

Ellene lifted her computer case from the table. "I need to get home, so I'll have to take my chances, I guess. I'll drive down there and wait."

Aunt Phyllis shook her head. "It could be a long wait. Why not wait here? Connor can call the ferry and check."

"Thanks, but I'd rather see for myself."

Pulling her cheek away from a chair back where she'd been listening, Caitlin rose and moved closer. "We could play games."

Ellene faced her with a sympathetic grin. "I'd love to play games, but not tonight."

Caitlin's expectant look fell. She plopped into a chair and lowered her head as if she'd been personally rejected.

Connor opened his mouth to say more, but he gave up. Ellene had always been one of the most obstinate women he'd ever met. Today was proof. "If it's hopeless, come back, will you?"

She slipped her arms into her jacket, flipped her dark hair over the collar and buttoned it. "I have confidence in the coast guard."

His shoulders sagged with her ridiculous comment. Stubborn. Stubborn. Stubborn. "Fine. Let me know when you have some plans ready, okay?"

"Sure," she said, grasping her laptop handle. "So nice to see you, Aunt Phyllis," she said, giving the woman a hug. "And Caitlin, I really enjoyed meeting you."

Caitlin lifted her gaze and shrugged her shoulder.

"I'll be in touch," she said, turning the doorknob and stepping outside.

The cold wind whipped through the open door, then vanished as she closed it.

Connor stared at the door a moment, waiting for it to reopen and Ellene to come back, but she didn't. When he turned around, his aunt Phyllis was shaking her head.

"Bullheaded, isn't she?"

Connor couldn't help but smile. "She has her moments, but she's a wonderful woman on good days."

"Why wouldn't she stay, Daddy?" Caitlin whined from her slouched pose on the chair, her arms folded across her chest.

"She has her reasons, Caitlin." He started to say he didn't know, but he did. Ellene couldn't let go of the past. He hadn't, either, not for many years.

"What reasons?"

"Caitlin, we don't always get our way. Sometimes people have their own plans." He glanced at his aunt and arched a brow. "And Ellene definitely has her own."

"For better or worse," Aunt Phyllis said.

For better or worse? Connor studied his aunt's expression, observing a sly grin that he recognized from her days of trying to play matchmaker for him.

"Don't push it, Aunt Phyllis," he said, grinning back. "I can always uninvite you to dinner."

Her grin faded. Then she recouped and laughed. "You wouldn't."

Connor arched a brow and didn't answer.

Her jaw set in determination, Ellene pulled away from Connor's house and headed toward the ferry. The setting sun had caused the temperature to drop and the roads that had once crunched beneath her tires had frozen into slippery ruts.

She gripped the wheel, thinking of the pleasant warmth of Connor's fireplace and the warmth of his smile. Shadows lengthened along the channel road, and at the turn, her car skidded toward a ditch until she wrestled her way back to the road, thankful for the blessing.

Her earlier line to appease Caitlin jumped into her thoughts. I'd love to live on an island. She shook her head. There wasn't a grain of truth in that statement, but if she'd been wise, tonight she could have stayed. Her stomach gnawed, recalling the aroma of the goulash. The place needed work, but it could be a cozy home for Caitlin, except for the when-things-happen issue.

How could people live in a location that cut them off from the rest of the world? The questions tossed in her thoughts as she recalled the sunny summer days by the lake, the fresh breeze from the water, the easygoing lifestyle so different from the tensions of her daily life.

She could picture the moon hanging over the water. More than in well-populated areas, stars filled the sky on the island, winking and blinking with their phantasmal splendor. It spelled romance.

Romance. She brushed away the thought.

The ferry dock rose into view as her spirits sank. No cars waiting, only a large sign. Ferry Closed Until Further Notice. She saw a man inside the small building, and she pulled into the ferry driveway. When she stepped from the car, the breeze had whipped into a bitter wind. It was March. Only in Michigan would this weather make sense.

"Ferry's closed," the man called from the building door.

"For how long?"

He shrugged and shook his head. "Not tonight, I can guarantee. Tomorrow doesn't look good, especially if this storm comes in that's heading this way." He gave a toss of his head. "It could be longer."

Ellene looked into the sky and saw the burdened slate-colored clouds. Winter storm. Just what she needed. Her shoulders sagged with the weight of the news. "Any hotels around here?"

He chuckled. "Not on the island."

"Rooms for rent? Bed and breakfasts?"

He shook his head. "You can rent cabins in the summer. Not now."

Her frustration flared as she climbed back into the car. She smacked the heel of her hand against the steering wheel, then backed out of the driveway and stopped along the edge of the road. She didn't want to go back and face Connor's I-told-you-so look. Connor. Even his name caused her pulse to skip. She'd tried forever to push the memories from her mind, but failed. Every man she had dated she'd compared to Connor.

Now after all these years, he had a daughter, a six-year-old who — She paused, counting on her fingers. They'd dated until nearly eight years ago. Connor truly hadn't wasted time. He'd dated Ellene forever, it seemed, so how could he fall in love with someone else that fast? She'd heard he'd met someone after only a few months. Gossip was never completely trustworthy, but could he really have loved another woman while Ellene's emotions burned for months . . . a year or more?

A sigh escaped her as she pulled her cell phone from her purse. She wanted to talk with someone, anyone who would understand. Her mother? No. Her father? That would be worse.

Christine Powers? Ten years older but like a big sister. They'd become friends at a fitness spa. Funny how friendships formed. They'd had dinner together one evening after a workout, talked about a new Tom Hanks movie they both wanted to see, and that was it — a friendship sprang up.

Ellene flipped through her address book until she found Christine's number, hoping she'd be home. Saturday night was date night for most single woman.

She listened to the ring, and when she was

about ready to hang up, Christine answered.

"Guess where I am?" Ellene said, after identifying herself.

"In Jamaica?"

"Don't I wish. Stranded on Harsens Island."

"Stranded?"

Ellene groaned out her story — Connor, Caitlin and the closed ferry. "Connor insisted I stay, but I couldn't?"

"You couldn't? Did you find a hotel?"

"None. Nothing."

"Then where are you?"

Christine's voice lifted with her question, and Ellene could picture the look on her face. "Sitting at the closed ferry landing."

"Hmm? And you're too proud to go back to Connor's."

"It's not that exactly." The truth flashed in her thoughts. "Okay, so I'm proud, but it's more than that. I'm still attracted to him, Christine, and I don't know what to do."

Christine's chuckle bounced from the phone. "Do I need to explain how uncontrollable emotions —"

"But I don't want to have feelings for Connor. I told you what happened with him and later Owen doing the same thing." Owen. Her chest tightened at the mistake she'd made with him. "I can't handle this now. How can I trust a man who hurt me so badly?"

"Did you ever wonder if you hurt him, Ellene?"

Her friend's question knocked her backward into the seat. "It's not what I'd planned. You know that. I thought —"

"Thinking has consequences. People handle rejection in different ways. You withdrew, and Connor rebounded. He found someone who loved him without expectations."

She pictured Connor running into the arms of another woman who thought he was perfect. Ellene realized that at one time she'd thought he was perfect. She had analyzed the relationship countless times. He loved her. She loved him, but she'd begun to feel she owned him. She'd wanted him to ignore his buddies to spend time with her. She'd even been upset when he cancelled a date because his mother had an emergency and needed him. Her emotions had swung from one extreme to the other — from deeply frustrated to a longing that defied her upbringing.

"Are you there?" Christine asked.

"Sorry. I was thinking."

"Are you thinking about the right things?"

"What do you mean right things?"

"The good times with Connor. Once you raked him over the coals for a year, I recall you telling me about his tenderness, his charm, his respect for your Christian morals, his uncanny way —"

"I remember, but that doesn't make up for —"

"I liked him. Do you remember those moonlight hayrides you told me about, walks through the woods in autumn, tobogganing in winter, swimming at Kensington Beach, picnics at Bloomer State Park, Franklin Cider Mill."

Ellene wanted to scream. She remembered all too well. "I called you to give me moral support, not to —"

Car lights flashed in her eyes. The vehicle slowed and her heart rose when she realized it was Connor.

"Connor's here, Christine."

"There, at the ferry landing?"

Ellene nodded, watching Connor climb from his SUV and head for the passenger side of her car.

"Ellene?"

"He's here, Christine. Thanks for listening. I know you meant well. I suppose I should think about the good times, but it only makes me sad."

"It doesn't have to," Christine said.

Connor rapped his knuckles against her locked door.

"I'll talk with you later?"

"Think about what I said. That's all I ask. You don't want to be sorry you missed a chance."

Missed a chance. A chance for what? Getting hurt again? She pressed the lock release on the door, and Connor pulled it open. The cold wind swished inside, sending a chill up her spine. "I will. Talk to you later." She disconnected as Connor closed the door.

A frown flashed across his face. "Boyfriend?"

"No." She slipped the phone into her purse. "The ferry's really closed."

"I know. I thought you'd come back."

She turned away from the sadness in his eyes. "I have no choice unless you know of a place for me to stay."

"Nothing on the island, but if you're not comfortable staying at the cottage, Aunt Phyllis invited you there. She has plenty of room and would love the company."

Why hadn't she thought of that? "That would work fine, Connor. Thanks. You know me and my upbringing." Guilt washed over her, thinking back, but she didn't want to deal with those memories now.

"I understand. I always have, Ellene."

"I know." She couldn't look at him.

"I have a big plate of goulash for you and a salad. You must be starving."

She nodded, trying to control the sensations that coiled around her heart. She wished he weren't so thoughtful. She could detest him better that way.

"Caitlin will be thrilled you're back. She went into pout mode after you left." He shook his head. "Everything that smacks of abandonment seems to tear her apart."

"Abandonment? You mean because I left?"

His eyes widened. "I didn't mean it was your fault. It's Caitlin. She opened up to you. She seemed more like herself than she has in days, but when she takes a chance and gets caught up in a relationship, the poor kid can't handle people saying good-bye."

His comment struck her like a rock. "Her mother's death. That makes sense."

"Yes, and I withdrew for a while. I tried not to, but I felt abandoned, too. What did I know about raising a four-year-old by myself? I had to cope with finding sitters and worrying about her care and needs. I felt guilty when I had to go somewhere if she couldn't go along. My life changed in the blink of an eye. I felt helpless and useless."

Ellene's chest tightened. "I can't imagine what you went through."

"It felt like punishment." He lifted his hand as if to stop her thoughts. "Not having to raise Caitlin alone, but having Melissa die so young. I wasn't the best husband in the world, Ellene. I —"

He stopped. She waited, her questions hanging on the threads of his words, but they seemed too personal to ask when he was apparently still grieving.

"Should we go back?" she asked.

"That's what I'm here for," he said, smiling as if he'd taken control of his emotion. "You go ahead, and I'll follow you."

He opened the door as she turned the key in the ignition, but the heater's warmth couldn't hold back the pesky cold.

"Drive carefully," he said, leaning back into the car. "Thanks for listening." He closed the door and hurried toward his car.

Thanks for listening. The poignant comment swelled in her chest like yeast in bread dough. Hearing his story, Ellene realized Connor had paid the price for any wrongdoing he'd done, if he'd done anything so wrong in the first place. Sorrow over-whelmed her. *Lord, help me to mend my ways and give me a kind heart toward him.*

CHAPTER FIVE

When a thread of sunlight slipped beneath the window shade, Connor rolled over and covered his eyes from the morning. Yet today offered him a different feeling, a new hope. He eased upward and inched open his eyes to look at the clock sitting on the nightstand. Though it was too early to get up, he longed to slip into jeans and a long-sleeved knit shirt and run next door to see Ellene — to assure himself she was still there, that she hadn't run off in the night or been only a hope-filled dream.

Though Ellene had refused the invitation to stay in his cottage, she'd accepted his aunt's offer. Knowing his aunt, she'd probably talked Ellene to sleep, but he felt grateful she'd given her a bed and, in the scheme of things, had given Connor another chance to make amends for the past. Now if he could garner the courage to tell her the truth.

71

When Ellene had agreed to work with him on the cottage renovations, an amazing opportunity had arisen, and Connor had prayed that God give him a way to spend some quality time with her. He hadn't considered an ice jam, but if that had been God's means of answering his prayer, Connor whispered a thank-you.

He rose on one elbow and ran his other hand through his hair, wondering if Ellene might soften her attitude. Last night when they'd returned from the ferry landing, she'd eaten a little but left for Aunt Phyllis's as fast as she could. He knew she wanted to avoid him, but Connor had other plans.

Connor gave up any further plans to sleep and pushed his hand against the mattress to hoist himself to a sitting position. He went to the window, lifted the shade and savored the morning. The new snow glinted from the ground, and across the channel the ice looked unyielding.

He bowed his head, praying that the ferry didn't run today, either. Then feeling guilty, Connor dressed quickly and crept into the kitchen so as not to wake Caitlin.

Only a couple eggs were in the refrigerator. With the ferry service down, he guessed the store in town would be sold out of eggs by the time he reached it. He found some bacon, but bacon and what? He grinned, remembering he'd recently purchased a box of pancake mix. That could last them a few days, if need be.

After putting on the coffee, Connor returned to his room, showered and dressed in fresh clothes, then crept upstairs to Caitlin's room and peeked inside. She lay curled into a ball, her tawny hair splayed across the pillow. Often he had assailed God for forcing him to be a single parent, but as always, seeing his daughter's flushed cheeks, her eyes closed and still, he gave thanks for the blessing.

Sunlight spread across her floor through the loose blinds, and Connor knew it would only be a short time before the bright rays would beguile her from her bed. He hoped her mood today would be better than yesterday's.

He returned to the kitchen and glanced through the side door toward his aunt's house. He figured she would be awake, but he hated to phone in case Ellene was still sleeping. He wanted to run over to invite her to breakfast, but he didn't want to leave Caitlin alone.

Disappointed, he turned from the door and spotted Caitlin standing by the staircase, rubbing her fists into her eyes. "The sun woke me up," she said, dragging into the room and plopping onto the sofa.

He glanced at the doorway, wondering if he dare run next door, then stopped himself. A good father should care more for the well-being of his child than for impressing an old girlfriend with breakfast. "How about getting dressed so we can go to Aunt Phyllis's for a minute."

She shook her head. "Don't want to."

He watched her attitude surface like grease on water. "Caitlin. I want to invite Ellene over for breakfast."

"She went home."

"No. She had to come back because the ferry wasn't running. You remember when Aunt Phyllis watched you while I went to find her?"

She nodded.

"Well, you fell asleep before we got back. I carried you up to bed."

Her eyes widened. "Ellene came back?"

"She's at Aunt Phyllis's."

"Why? She could have stayed with us."

Her eyes searched his. "Because it's not proper for a single woman to stay in the house with a single man."

"I'm here. You never think I'm important." She tossed herself back against the sofa.

"You're the most important person in my

life, Caitlin." He walked to her and sat on the edge of the cushion beside her, but she drew away. "Please don't be moody today. I invited Ellene to stay. She didn't think it was proper. You should ask her."

She perked up and eyed him. "She's really next door?"

"She is. Get dressed and we'll invite her to breakfast."

Caitlin bounded from the seat and darted up the stairs while Connor filled a coffee cup and took a drink. The warm liquid radiated through him, banishing his skepticism with confidence. Ellene seemed to work wonders on Caitlin. Maybe he could — He stopped himself. Wishes and longings led to disappointment. He wasn't going there.

In moments, Caitlin's footsteps pounded down the stairs. He grinned, seeing her flowery tights and striped shirt. She'd inherited his bad taste in color combinations, he feared. She grasped her jacket off the chair where she'd tossed it yesterday and slipped her arms into the sleeves as she headed for him. "Let's go, Daddy. Where's your coat?"

"You're eager," he said, trying not to grin at her enthusiasm. Connor found his jacket, slid it on and zipped the front. "Let's go, speedy."

"I'm not speedy," Caitlin said, joining him at the door.

"You are when you want to be."

The snow cracked beneath Connor's feet as they broke through the icy crust. March. While most of the country was rejoicing in flower blossoms and leafing trees, he trudged across the frozen ground.

Caitlin walked beside him, her small feet slipping over the icy ridges as she grabbed his jacket for support.

"Careful," Connor warned.

She only giggled and skidded ahead of him to his aunt's door. She gave a knock then turned the knob and vanished inside before Connor caught up with her.

When he stepped inside, the warmth of the house struck him along with the scent of food. Pepper, his aunt's terrier, let out a yip and danced around his feet. He liked animals, but this one drove him to distraction.

Caitlin knelt and pulled the bouncing terrier into her arms while Connor slipped past. Disappointment rose as the smell of sausage let him know that he wouldn't be making Ellene breakfast.

"Good morning," he said, his gaze drifting past his aunt to look for Ellene.

"She's in the bathroom," she said.

He flinched, realizing he'd been too obvious. "I thought maybe she was still sleeping."

"Nope. We're about to have breakfast. I can toss in a couple more eggs if you haven't eaten."

"I made coffee. I thought I'd cook breakfast."

"Too late. It's cooked." She tilted her head toward fluffy-looking eggs beside sausage popping in the frypan.

"I'll have some scrambled eggs," Caitlin said, before he could stop her.

"We're having pancakes," Connor said.

"I don't want pancakes. I want to eat here with Ellene."

He wanted to remind her that people didn't always get what they wanted, but he saved his breath. Among the mixture of aromas, Connor didn't smell coffee. He eyed the empty pot.

"I'm out of coffee. If you made some, why not bring it over while I throw in a couple more eggs."

Connor's attention shifted from Aunt Phyllis to Caitlin. He let his own breakfast plans fade. Without a comment, he opened the door and stepped outside into the cold.

As the damp chill rolled up his spine, so did his concern. Connor's old dreams were coming to life again when Ellene had stepped back into his world. And if she turned away from him, the cold rejection would be far worse than any winter storm.

He reached the cottage, grasped the coffeepot, and headed back, his mind rocked by confusion. Why had he allowed himself to think that he and Ellene could make amends and rekindle their old relationship? She'd hurt him once, and he'd rebounded with so much fervor, he'd changed his life. Except for Caitlin's birth, he'd made a grave error.

When he opened the door, Connor side-stepped the dog trying to make an escape to the outside before he came to a halt.

Ellene sat at the kitchen table, dressed in a lilac knit top that belonged to his aunt. On her feet, she wore socks and a pair of his aunt's slippers.

As he lifted his gaze, Ellene smiled. "I was not equipped for a sleepover." She wiggled her feet showing off the big fuzzy footwear. "Any news on the ferry?"

"I haven't heard, but I'll call."

"I checked," Aunt Phyllis said. "Nothing. Not expected to run today."

"But —"

"You can't fight nature," Aunt Phyllis said. "We'll make the best out of it. It's Sunday.

After breakfast, we'll have church."

Connor felt his brow wrinkle. "Have church?"

"We can't get over to our church in Algonac, can we?"

"No, but —"

"Did you ever hear the Lord add *but* to his sentences? Nope. You never did. We'll worship right here."

Connor gazed around the kitchen before his focus landed in the living room. Worship could happen anywhere, he supposed. "That's fine as long as you don't make us sing."

Ellene lowered her head and covered her mouth as if hiding a grin.

"So, let's eat." Aunt Phyllis waved them to the chairs, and Connor did as he'd been told. He'd learned years ago that his aunt was difficult to sway when she had something on her mind.

Connor watched Ellene dig into the breakfast. She remained quiet, concentrating on her toast as she used it to push the eggs onto her fork.

He watched Caitlin follow Ellene's every move as if entranced by the woman. He had to admit he was mesmerized himself, yet warnings zinged through his head like buckshot. Could he ever trust her again?

Aunt Phyllis chattered on about everything from past emergencies on the island to her oil bill, and finally she quieted.

She remained so quiet Connor felt nervous. "Is something bothering you, Aunt Phyllis?"

She sat a moment in silence, then shook her head. "Nothing important. I'm wondering how the oil will last if we're holed up here for too long. The tank's due a refill."

"We won't let you freeze." But her comment triggered his own set of concerns. He'd already noticed he had only a few eggs. "Maybe I should get home and see what we need. I can take a run to the grocery in town before everyone else buys the place out."

"After our worship, Connor. The store doesn't open until noon on Sunday."

He glanced at his watch, knowing she was right. Still he hesitated. He definitely needed to stock his pantry.

When breakfast ended, Ellene volunteered to clean the kitchen while his aunt retrieved her Bible. Connor carried dishes to the sink, but Ellene shook her head. "I'll do this."

He felt as if he'd been dismissed by her businesslike tone. If Ellene wanted to play hard to get, he could do the same. Connor strode into the living room and sank into an overstuffed chair.

Caitlin followed Aunt Phyllis from her bedroom, carrying her Bible and a small tape player. Connor did a double take. He'd been joking about the hymns, and now he wondered.

Soon Ellene entered the living room and settled on the sofa. Caitlin skittered from her spot beside him and bounded to Ellene's side.

Aunt Phyllis sat across from them, slid her legs on a footstool and opened the Bible. "Let's begin with prayer," she said.

Connor tried not to frown as he glanced at Ellene who'd already closed her eyes and folded her hands. He bowed his head and listened as his aunt prayed a blessing on their worship and on them.

When she'd finished, Connor raised his head and eyed his aunt. Although he appreciated her attempt to worship in their home, something prodded him to think she also had an ulterior motive. Was it the look on her face or the sparkle in her eye that gave her away?

"Today we'll listen to the story of Jacob and his coat." She flipped through the page, then adjusted the Bible.

Connor had never been a Bible scholar, but he knew that the story of Joseph went on for many chapters in the book of Genesis, and his mind grappled with her purpose in sharing this story since he knew Aunt Phyllis always had a purpose for everything.

"Genesis 37, verse 1," she said, " 'Jacob lived in the land where his father had stayed, the land of Canaan. This is the account of Jacob. Joseph, a young man of seventeen, was tending the flocks with his brothers. . . .' "

Connor leaned back, listening to the hum of his aunt's voice as she read the story of Joseph's dreams, his brothers' envy of his father's love, symbolized by his ornamented robe, and how he was sold into slavery.

"Genesis, chapter 39," Aunt Phyllis continued, " 'Now Joseph had been taken down to Egypt.' "

Connor began to squirm. Then his knee began to jiggle, and he straightened it to control his movement. He looked at Ellene and though she was listening, he caught her in a large yawn. She covered her mouth and avoided his eyes.

Caitlin had settled back against the sofa pillow, her eyes weighted with glazed sleep.

The story continued as Joseph gained prominence in Pharaoh's eyes by interpreting dreams that saved the land from the famine until Joseph was made in charge of the whole land. In chapter 42, Jacob sent Joseph's brothers to Egypt to buy grain and each time they went before Joseph they were unaware that he was their brother.

Finally in chapter 45, Aunt Phyllis breathed a sigh and gazed at them. "Don't fall asleep on me now, here's the ending."

Connor widened his eyes, hoping to look attentive and wondering why his aunt had chosen such a long reading from the Bible. When he looked at Ellene, her focus had shifted to the ceiling, and she was twirling a strand of hair between her fingers.

Aunt Phyllis lifted the Bible higher and continued. " 'Then Joseph said to his brothers, "Come close to me." When they had done so, he said, "I am your brother Joseph, the one you sold into Egypt! And now, do not be distressed and do not be angry with yourselves for selling me here, because it was to save lives that God sent me ahead of you." ' "

When she finished the chapter, she closed the Bible and looked at Connor, then at Ellene and back to Connor. "Did you hear that? Joseph threw his arms around Benjamin and wept, and then he kissed all his brothers and wept over them."

"I heard that," Connor said.

"Do you know what it means?" But instead of looking at him, she turned her gaze directly at Ellene.

"It's the story of God's love for a family," Ellene said.

"It's the story of forgiveness," Aunt Phyllis said. "His brothers betrayed Joseph, they almost left him for dead, but instead they sold him into slavery. All for envy. But Joseph forgave his brothers. He showed the greatest love to them even after they'd done the unthinkable." She shifted in her chair and placed the Bible on the table. "It's all about forgiveness."

Connor eyed Ellene and saw an uneasy look on her face. She'd obviously realized his aunt's purpose in sharing that particular lesson.

Aunt Phyllis rose from the chair and popped a tape into the tape recorder, then pushed the button. A familiar praise hymn filled the air. The music seemed to ease the tension, and when Connor looked at Ellene, she smiled.

CHAPTER SIX

Ellene had managed to smile at Connor, but inside she winced with his aunt's lesson. Last night the woman had grilled her about her breakup with Connor, and today she'd used her Bible reading — her long Bible reading — to bring home the lesson.

Her father had tried the same tack with his lesson of forgiveness. Ellene didn't want to harbor a grudge. Still it seemed more than forgiveness to her. She admitted she'd been wrong, too, but every time she recalled how quickly Connor had fallen into another woman's arms — even married her and gave her a child — the years she and Connor had spent together became a charade.

"I suppose I'll have to work from here," Ellene said, wanting to make it perfectly clear that she didn't plan to use the situation for fun. "I'll call my father and explain."

Connor's expression tensed. "How can you work from here?"

"I have a phone and a laptop. I can manage for a couple of days." Her head rang with Aunt Phyllis's ominous declaration from the day before about the downed ferry service. *It lasts a few hours or a few days. Sometimes two or three weeks at the most.*

"Are you okay?" Connor's voice pierced her thoughts.

"I'm fine. Just thinking of what I have to do." She rose from the table. "I'll get my laptop and then make a few calls."

All three of them gaped at her as if she'd ruined the party.

"Please, you can all go back to whatever you do. Don't let me bother you."

"You're no bother," Aunt Phyllis said. "Connor and I need to take stock of what we have and what we need. The store opens in a half hour, and we'll need to pick up what we can. You never know."

You never know. The phrase latched onto Phyllis's earlier statement and knocked the breath out of Ellene. She turned her back and walked from the room, trying to ignore the dire remark. When she reached her room, she sat on the edge of the bed, realizing her mind was far from work.

Noises sounded from the other room — cabinet doors opening and closing, the outside door banging, Caitlin whining about something and finally Connor announcing his aunt's oil tank was nearly empty.

While she tried to set her mind on work tasks, the empty oil tank dwelled in her thoughts. Was Connor's empty, too? Would they freeze before rescue came? She felt like a novice mountain climber stranded on Mount Everest.

Ellene dismissed the vexing thoughts, dug into her handbag and pulled out her cell phone. She pushed in the numbers, letting the phone ring. On the third buzz, the secretary's voice came from the answering machine stating business hours. "We're open Monday through Friday from . . ."

Today was Sunday. She'd just tolerated Aunt Phyllis's down-her-throat sermon. How had she forgotten? She hit the menu button on her cell and punched her parents' phone number. Voice mail kicked in. She pushed the off switch. She refused to talk to voice mail when she wanted a human.

She plopped onto the edge of the bed, her frustration pounding in her head. So today was Sunday, a day of rest. Not with her stranded here with Connor and his family. How could she rest? She needed to keep her guard up at all times.

She opened the laptop and sat it on the

nightstand, then twisted her body around to use the keyboard and opened a customer folder. At least she could accomplish a few tasks without the interruption of her phone ringing or someone wanting her to go out on the road for an estimate.

Within a few minutes, her back ached from its contorted position at the keyboard, and though she'd read the document over twice, her concentration was nil. Once again, she'd have to let her pride fall by the wayside and admit today was not a day to work.

She turned off the computer and straightened her spine. The house seemed quieter. She rose and walked to the bedroom window. Outside, she saw Connor tapping on his oil tank and then checking the gauge. She tried to read his expression, but all she could tell was that he hadn't frowned.

He opened his cabin door and went inside, and Ellene stayed there, too stubborn to go into the other room to see what was happening. In a moment, she heard the side door close and saw Aunt Phyllis and Caitlin crossing the slippery distance to join Connor.

She felt utterly alone.

Her breath fogged the windowpane, and she brushed it away, wondering what they were doing at Connor's. Was he setting a warm blaze in the fireplace or making Caitlin hot chocolate? She would enjoy a tasty treat, too.

The window hazed again, and she dropped the curtain, then glanced down at the fuzzy slippers and purple top she'd borrowed from Connor's aunt. She found her shoes beneath the bed, slipped them on, and picked up her jacket. She could, at least, find out what they were doing? Maybe they needed her help.

She snorted at the idea. What help would she be on an island she didn't know with a man she wanted to avoid? But right now, she didn't want to avoid anyone. Loneliness had won over her pride.

Ellene shoved her arm into her jacket as she left the bedroom and made her way to the side door. No one used the front door, she'd learned. When she stepped outside, the bitter wind nipped at her back as she trudged through the brittle snow.

At Connor's she raised her hand to knock, then thought better of it and opened the door.

Connor spun around in surprise. "I thought you were working."

"It's Sunday. I forgot."

A grin tilted the edge of his mouth. "Then

welcome to our scavenger hunt."

"What?"

"We're deciding how we can pool resources, then we're going shopping. You can come along if you'd like."

If you'd like. Like, what else did she have to do? No, I'd rather stay here and watch the ground freeze. Having better thoughts, she shrugged, hoping to look noncommittal. "Anything I can do?"

"You can play a game with me?" Caitlin said, appearing from the bathroom with Aunt Phyllis behind her.

"Toilet paper," his aunt said, "and we'd better hurry." She seemed to notice Ellene, because her eyes widened. "Thought you were working."

"It's Sunday," Ellene said again.

"Good, then come along." She motioned for them to head out the door.

Connor didn't flinch. He strode to the door as if Aunt Phyllis were an army sergeant. Caitlin latched onto Ellene's hand, and they stepped outside.

"Don't anyone walk away from this car without carrying a bag."

Connor grinned at his aunt's command as they climbed from the SUV in his driveway.

He opened the hatch and doled out grocery bags, leaving the heaviest for himself.

The store had been crowded, as he'd expected. When he'd arrived outside the market, cars had already begun to line up waiting for the store to open so they could stock their pantries just in case.

Ellene had joined them, and she'd sat in the back with Caitlin, attempting to maintain her business persona while being barraged by Caitlin's chatter, but Connor saw she was having problems. He'd chuckled earlier when she'd suddenly appeared at his house, remembering it was Sunday and the office was closed. How could she have forgotten Aunt Phyllis's lengthy sermon?

"I can't believe the ferry still isn't running," Ellene said, snatching the paper bag from his arms. "You should have warned me."

"How did I know?" he asked, getting nothing more in return than an arched eyebrow and a sneer.

When he'd handed the last small package to Caitlin, Connor lifted the two heavier bags into his arms. The store didn't have everything they'd put on the list, but he'd grabbed eggs, milk and cheese, and a few packages of meat before the cases were nearly empty.

Ellene had purchased a few items of her own, he'd noticed when they arrived at the checkout counter — pads of paper, crayons, childproof scissors and he couldn't tell what else. Apparently Caitlin had helped her shop, and Ellene's thoughtfulness touched his heart.

Still he feared for Caitlin. She'd opened up to Ellene in the short time she'd been there, and he worried about her reaction when Ellene left for home. He'd noticed a tender look in Ellene's eyes when she spoke with Caitlin. He guessed she liked Caitlin, too, but he wasn't confident that she truly understood how devastating her departure could be for his daughter. Part of him wanted to get Ellene away from them before Caitlin was hurt — before *he* was hurt again.

"Where do you want this?" Ellene asked, piling canned goods onto the table.

He motioned to the cabinets. "The longest door is the pantry. You'll see where it goes."

She carried the products to the shelves while he stowed the dairy and meat in the refrigerator.

Aunt Phyllis stood beside the door where she'd left a bag of dog food. "I'll head back home. Pepper needs to eat."

Ellene looked up from the canned goods. "I'll be over shortly."

Connor felt the impact of her comment when he saw Caitlin's face, and he longed to say something but didn't, not in front of his daughter.

"Where are the cookies?" Caitlin asked, nosing into the empty bags.

"Cookies?" He realized that was an item they'd forgotten. "I'm sorry, Caitlin. We didn't buy cookies."

She stomped her foot. "But you promised."

He eyed Ellene hoping she'd say something about the crayons and paper she'd bought. He assumed they were for Caitlin.

She didn't say a word, but shifted the canned goods from one shelf to another as if she were alphabetizing them.

Caitlin tossed herself onto the sofa and smothered her face in the cushion. Her mumbled protests pierced the quiet.

Ellene closed the pantry door and faced him. "What's wrong?"

"We forgot the cookies."

"You promised," Caitlin wailed, turning her head so her words were clear and loud.

"We don't always get what we want, Caitlin. I've told you that. I'm sorry."

"But you promised," she said.

"Promises are important," Ellene whispered as she passed him. She sat on the arm of the sofa and looked down at Caitlin. "You know what's more fun than buying cookies?"

Caitlin's sobs softened. "What?" She hiccuped the word.

"Baking cookies," Ellene said.

Caitlin lifted her moist eyes and looked at her. "I've never baked cookies."

"You haven't? But that's the most fun."

Connor watched aghast as Ellene soothed his daughter. Why hadn't he thought about baking cookies? He gave the chair leg a soft kick. Because he wasn't a woman, that's why. Women thought of cookies and ribbons and crayons. Men didn't.

"Let's see if we have flour and things to make them. Okay?" Ellene said, giving Connor a frantic look.

He shrugged, hoping they had what she needed.

As she looked inside the cabinets, she brought out sugar, peanut butter, a flour bag that looked nearly empty. Then she grabbed a cookbook sitting on an open bookshelf and flipped through the pages.

"I'll run over to see if Aunt Phyllis has the other things we need." She gave Connor a questioning look as if asking why he hadn't bought flour and who knows what so they could make cookies.

He didn't try to respond.

She grabbed her jacket and vanished through the doorway, leaving a nippy breeze along with her cold shoulder.

Connor felt disappointed in himself and disappointed in Caitlin. He couldn't allow her to behave this way, and he was at a loss as to what to do.

He sidled across the room and sat on the edge of the sofa near Caitlin's feet. "Cait, I'm sorry, but we're sort of stranded here, and sometimes things don't happen the way we want them. You can't throw a fit every time things don't go your way."

She looked at him with sad eyes. "But Daddy, you promised."

"I know, but —" But. He recalled Aunt Phyllis saying God didn't use the word. "I forgot, Cait. I made a mistake."

"You told me God makes promises and He doesn't forget, but if He's our Father then maybe He'll forget, too."

Her logic stung him. "No, Caitlin, God is different. He's almighty and bigger than any human. He'd never forget His promises. God says, 'My eyes and my heart will always be there.' That means He is always watching you and always caring for you."

"Is love in the heart, Daddy?"

"I think so."

"When you die, does your heart lose all its love?"

His chest tightened with her question. How could he answer that? When the body died, the heart died, but love? Did love die or did it just go with the soul to heaven? "Your mom loves you even now, Caitlin. She's up in heaven loving you with all her heart."

She eyed Connor as if weighing what he'd said. "Does she know I miss her?"

The questions — so many with impossible answers. "If she knew how much we missed her, she'd be sad, I think, but I'm sure she knows you love her, because that would make her happy."

A faint grin touched her lips. "Everyone is happy in heaven."

"That's right. I promise you that, Caitlin, and that's a promise I can keep."

She gave a gentle nod and pushed herself into a seated position, then reached up to wrap her arms around his waist. Connor drew her closer, smelling the fragrance of his child and praying to God to calm his daughter's heart.

They were still embracing when the door opened, and Ellene came inside, stomping clumps of snow from her shoes.

"It's melting a little. That could be good news with the ferry service."

"Could be," he said, hating to tell her that it took more than a little sunshine to break up the ice jam. Often it melted a little during the day, fusing it together even more strongly in the evening when it became colder.

"Did you find what you needed?" he asked.

"I think so."

She set a bag of flour and a container of baking powder or soda onto the counter. He could never remember which was which.

Ellene pulled a mixing bowl from the cabinet and lifted a wooden spoon from a crockery container beside the stove. "Ready to make cookies, Caitlin?"

Caitlin unwound her arms from Connor and scooted off the sofa. She pulled up a small stool his mother must have used to reach items in the upper cabinets, and it made Caitlin just the right height at the counter.

He watched as Ellene showed her how to measure the ingredients, and Caitlin forgot all about his promise as she mixed the peanut butter and milk into the flour and sugar.

His heart stirred watching Ellene beside his daughter. Had life turned out differently, Caitlin could have been their child. He remembered how Ellene had talked about "one day when they had children." She'd wanted a daughter for her and a son for him, as if they could divide their love and energy into two little beings. He knew what she meant, but the idea always made him smile.

"Not too much," Ellene said.

Connor focused on the cookie making. Caitlin placed a small glob of dough in her hands, rolling it into a ball.

Ellene looked at him and grinned. "Her hands are so warm, she's turning the dough into mush."

He could see what she meant as Caitlin pulled her hands apart and the glob stuck to both palms.

"We'll have to put flour on your hands," Ellene said, showing more patience than Connor had ever seen her display.

Caitlin giggled as her gooey hands became white with flour. They tried again, and this time Caitlin dropped a round ball of dough onto the cookie sheet.

When they were finished, Ellene took a fork and showed Caitlin how to make crisscross marks on the dough. Connor had become so intrigued that he'd risen and stood over them, admiring the even marks etching each cookie.

"Good job," he said, kissing Caitlin's warm cheek.

She grinned and licked some dough from her fingers. "Want some? It's good."

"I'll wait until it's a cookie," he said, chuckling at her offer.

By the time Ellene had cleaned the kitchen counter and placed the dirty dishes into the dishwasher, the scent of peanut butter cookies filled the room. The fragrance seemed to mesmerize them all. Ellene had forgotten her frustration at being stranded and had given him a smile when Caitlin stood close to the oven as if waiting for the door to open and the cookies to come floating out.

"Is it time yet?" she asked.

"Wait for the beep. I set the timer." She chuckled as she pulled three glasses from the cabinet. "Warm cookies are nice with milk. Who wants some?"

Connor's hand shot into the air as did Caitlin's. Ellene lifted hers, too, then laughed at herself before pulling the gallon carton from the refrigerator.

When the glasses were filled, the buzzer sounded, and Ellene lifted the cookie sheets from the oven.

Caitlin licked her lips as she stood nearby watching the process.

"They have to cool a couple minutes before we can take them from the pan."

"Why?" Caitlin asked.

"They're still soft and they'll fall apart. You don't want to eat cookie crumbs do you?"

Caitlin licked her lips again and nodded.

Connor and Ellene laughed at the same time. The feeling of friendship and warmth — not only from the fresh-baked cookies but from their camaraderie — filled him with pleasure. Why couldn't they always be this way?

Ellene grasped three pieces of paper towel and plopped two soft cookies onto each sheet, then handed one to Caitlin and one to him. They sat at the kitchen table and when Caitlin took her first bite, her face glowed.

Connor rubbed his belly. "Yummy. These are better than the ones in the store."

"You don't get home-baked cookies from your dad, do you?" he asked Caitlin.

Caitlin shook her head, crumbs dotting her lips. "But you give me other things. Ellene gives me cookies."

His chest swelled, seeing his daughter so happy and normal, and his thanks went to

Ellene for making them almost like a real family.

Real family. The words snapped at him. Don't fool yourself, Connor. This is no more real than your engagement years ago. At a moment's notice, Ellene can walk out the door and leave you and Caitlin catching your breath. She did it once, and she can do it again.

CHAPTER SEVEN

Ellene woke with Pepper curled up against her chest, breathing into her face. She scooted the dog away from her, but the terrier wriggled back and licked her cheek.

She sat upright, lifting the dog and lowering him to the floor. She liked animals but getting that personal was a little uncomfortable.

She swung her legs over the mattress edge and ran her fingers through her tangled hair. She felt a mess without her own clothes, and she knew if this didn't end soon, she'd have to go into town and find a few personal items. She was grateful Connor's aunt had given her a toothbrush and loaned her a nightgown and a couple of knit tops.

How did she get herself into this mess? She shook her head, amazed that somehow fate had brought Connor and her back under the same roof — and stranded, to beat all.

Or was it fate?

Yesterday had seemed too comfortable. Her heart went out to Caitlin, and though she knew the child's reaction to the forgotten cookies was over the top, she understood. Every broken promise felt as if someone were forsaking her — the same way she felt about her mother's absence.

But Ellene didn't want to get caught in the trap. Each moment her concern grew deeper for the child, and Connor was right. The little girl had latched onto her like paste to paper. As soon as the ferry service opened, Ellene knew she would be on her way home.

Home. She dug into her bag and pulled out her cell phone, then glanced at her watch, surprised at the time. For some reason, on the island, she slept more soundly, but she still woke early. Her father often went into the office early. She turned on her phone and dialed. He answered, as she'd hoped.

"Dad."

"Ellene? What's wrong?"

"I won't be in today."

She heard a pause, then his low grumble. "Why not?"

"I'm stranded."

"Stranded?"

"On Harsens Island."

"You're kidding."

She assured him she wasn't and gave him the details. "I'll get away as soon as the ferry service opens."

"Don't take chances sitting there in the cold."

She was endangering herself more by staying at Connor's. "I won't."

"Connor's stranded there, too?"

"Connor, his aunt Phyllis and Connor's daughter, Caitlin. Oh, and Pepper the terrier."

Her father chuckled. "Are you getting along okay?"

"With Pepper or Connor?" She grinned at her question. "Pepper's a bed hog."

"Sounds like you're fine. I'm pleased to hear you've forgiven Connor. It's about time."

She winced.

"Send my best to him and get back when you can. I'll hold off your clients."

"I'll do as much as possible from the laptop."

"Good girl. See you soon."

"I hope," she said.

After she hung up, she sat a moment, thinking of what her father had said. *It's about time.* But she hadn't forgiven him, and even if she could, she wouldn't trust him.

Ellene knew she needed to safeguard her heart. If she spent time at Aunt Phyllis's house, she could get some e-mail correspondence answered and do some figures on a couple of projects that were due when she got back.

An easier feeling spread over Ellene. She rose and headed for the shower. Warm water washed away her anxiety, and she felt more determined to stay away from Connor. In the process, she'd be certain not to upset Caitlin when she left.

After dressing, Ellene headed into the kitchen and faltered in the doorway. Caitlin sat at the table, eating a piece of toast. "I came over to play," she said.

"I can't play today, Caitlin. I have work to do."

The child's lip stuck out for a moment, and then drew back in. "I'll watch you."

Ellene closed her eyes a moment to calm her thoughts. "Won't your daddy miss you?"

She shook her head. "Aunt Phyllis is babysitting me while daddy runs some errands."

Ellene glanced toward Connor's aunt.

She turned from the stove. "He went to the hardware for batteries and candles. The electrical lines are icing over, and that can mean we may have some downed lines."

Dandy. Now she'd be stranded with Connor in candlelight. *Heavenly Father, what is happening here?* "I hope it doesn't come to that," she said, trying to sound casual for Aunt Phyllis's sake.

"We'll survive."

You may, but will I? "Speaking of errands," Ellene said, "if the ferry doesn't open soon, I'll need to find a store to buy some clothes."

"There's a couple nice shops in town," Phyllis said. "Stores open about ten, I think."

"Have you heard anything new about the ferry?"

"Still closed. I called this morning."

Ellene kept her mouth shut. She strode to the coffeemaker and grabbed a cup from the hook, then poured. The acrid scent told her the coffee had been made awhile ago, but she added milk and took a sip. Strong, but tolerable.

"Would you like some eggs?" Phyllis asked.

"No thanks. I'm not really hungry."

Caitlin continued to watch her with wide eyes, apparently hoping she'd give in and entertain her.

"Where are the paper and crayons I bought you?"

"Over there." She gave a little toss of her head.

Ellene noticed the items on a chair seat where Caitlin's coat hung on the back. "How about drawing a picture and coloring it while I do some work?"

Caitlin thought about the suggestion, then slid off the chair and brought back the pad of paper and crayons, settling as near as possible to Ellene.

While Caitlin concentrated on the drawing, Ellene opened the laptop and found an outlet to plug it into. She opened her software program and clicked a correspondence folder, then opened the first file and scanned the contents.

Ellene heard the scrape of a chair leg and glanced up. Aunt Phyllis sat adjacent to her, sipping a coffee and eyeing her as if she had something to say.

Ellene smiled and went back to her work, hoping to discourage conversation. Pepper dodged in and out of her legs, which was distracting enough.

"This is you," Caitlin said, turning the letter-size notepad toward her so she could see the picture. The child had drawn a stick figure with squiggles of dark curls and big fuzzy slippers.

"Very nice. Thank you," Ellene said, turning back to the computer.

"You can keep it."

"Great. I'll get it when I'm finished."

"Speaking of finished," Phyllis said, "what happened between you and Connor to break off your engagement?"

The question smacked Ellene between the eyes. She sat dumbfounded, trying to decide how to answer the question or how to avoid answering with Caitlin present.

"Things happen," she said after a grand pause.

"What things? You two seemed like peas in a pod."

"Maybe that was the problem. We were too close."

Phyllis's eyes narrowed. "You can't be too close. The Bible says, 'For this reason a man will leave his father and mother and be united to his wife, and they will become one flesh.' One flesh is pretty close."

Ellene felt stymied. She sensed no answer would make Connor's aunt happy. "We argued, I guess. It was so long ago."

"Any relationship is made up of differing opinions. Arguments are healthy. They keep a person on his toes, and they teach patience. Remember the Lord says to be humble and gentle; be patient, bearing with one another in love. I don't think you worked hard enough."

Worked hard enough? "I know relationships aren't always perfect, but they should be close to perfect."

Aunt Phyllis pursed her lips. "Relationships are difficult, but God said that it's not good for man to be alone. He meant woman, too. Life's too lonely without a partner."

"I've done okay by myself."

"You think so?"

Ellene felt her eyes widen. "I'm happy with my work. I do my job well."

"The Lord expects the wife to work for her husband. She works late into the night and makes a good home for her family so her husband is respected."

"What about the wife?"

"She's loved."

Ellene lowered her head like a child being punished. She didn't like being attacked — not attacked exactly — she felt cornered. "It just wasn't meant to be with Connor and me."

"Don't be so sure."

Ellene glanced at Phyllis and then Caitlin. The child appeared focused on her drawing, to Ellene's relief. "Why would you say that?"

"How do you think you got here?"

"I asked my father the same question. Connor asked for me. He said he trusted my work."

"I don't mean that. You're stranded on the island. Why did that happen?"

Awareness prickled up Ellene's arms. "The ice jammed."

"Who jammed the ice?" She lifted her index finger and pointed toward the ceiling.

Ellene followed the direction of her finger and stared at the white paint above her head. God? Had God really done this to her?

Caitlin's head had tilted upward toward the ceiling, too, as if expecting to see something there.

God, this isn't funny.

Connor paced his cottage, amazed at the envy he felt. Caitlin practically lived at his aunt's where Ellene had holed herself up, he knew, to avoid him. They had to talk. He hadn't wanted to get into all the details of their breakup, but maybe admitting his weakness would strengthen their friendship. Right now, he'd be grateful for that.

The snow drifted down as he stepped

outside, and the temperature had not let up. The ice jam was firmer than it had been. Ellene's escape seemed thwarted at every turn.

When he knocked and opened his aunt's door, Pepper shot from the house like a missile. Connor grabbed for the dog's collar, missed and slipped to the ground as his ire rose. "You dumb dog," he shouted.

Pepper skidded to a stop and bounded back, his tongue swiping at Connor's face.

"Get away from me, you mutt."

Laughter billowed from the house, and Connor looked up and saw Caitlin watching him while holding open the storm door. Before he could rise, she was joined by his aunt and Ellene.

His fall had served one positive purpose. Ellene grinned at him as he struggled to rise on the slippery ground. Pepper was still nearby, so Connor captured him and hooked the chain in the yard on his collar before going inside.

"You need to get a fence around this place, Aunt Phyllis, if you're going to keep that dog. He'll be out on the road and gone before you know it." That idea didn't sound bad to Connor, but he knew his aunt would be in a tizzy, and he had to weigh one evil against the other.

Aunt Phyllis ignored his plea as she studied the thermostat. "I turned this down to conserve oil, but it's too cold in here. I'm afraid the oil will run out, and I don't want the pipes to freeze."

After he'd checked the meter a few days earlier, Connor had figured her oil supply wouldn't last, and he suspected they would have to pool resources. He prayed he had enough oil to keep his cottage warm until the channel opened.

"Let me check," he said. "Caitlin held the door wide open. Maybe it's just a chill from outside."

"I don't think so," she said, "I turned it down really low."

"I'll look," he said, reaching for the door handle and stepping outside.

As he headed for the tank, the terrier skipped around his feet until he ran out of chain. When Connor eyed the meter, it read very low. He eyed the mutt, realizing that not only Aunt Phyllis and Ellene would now be his house guests, but the irritating dog.

It wasn't that he didn't like animals. He did. He liked dogs — just not ones who licked his face and who tried to make an escape every time a door opened.

"Bad news," he said, stepping inside. "Time to consolidate. You'll have to move over to my place, and we'll leave this very low and have to pray your pipes don't freeze."

He sidled a look at Ellene and saw her tense expression. Now, he'd never have a chance to talk unless he could get her away without Caitlin or his aunt around. The possibility seemed dubious.

"Sounds like a good idea," his aunt said. "We'll get our things and be over. I'm stiff as a board with this cold."

She wasn't the only thing stiff as a board, he noted as he looked at Ellene's rigid stance. It had dawned on him she was trying with every ounce of strength to stay aloof, but he saw in her eyes, she was losing ground. Maybe God had found a way to intercede. Connor longed to hear her admit she was at fault for their breakup and not him.

Remorse struck Connor without warning. He'd talked with her about Caitlin's admiration of her and the possible effect. Could she be protecting Caitlin as much as herself? The question wavered in his thoughts.

Connor left and headed to the house. He'd have to work out sleeping arrangements. He could give Ellene his bed, let Aunt Phyllis sleep with Caitlin, and he'd have the sofa. Connor pictured his lengthy frame scrunched on the sofa, and for the first time since the storm, he hoped the ferry service reopened soon.

Ellene put away the dinner dishes and occasionally glanced at Caitlin, whose nose was pressed against the windowpane.

"It's still snowing," Caitlin said, her voice beginning to sound whiny. Ellene had come to know that tone and longed to find a better way for the child to express her wants.

Ellene weighed what she knew. Anticipating Caitlin's desires might be a boon to solving the problem. If Caitlin realized people understood her wishes, the child might learn that she only needed to express what she wanted without whining.

"Does that mean you'd like to play in the snow?"

Caitlin did a slow turn. "To make a snowman."

"It's too cold," Connor said, reaching for the TV remote to change the station.

Ellene gave Caitlin a wink and wandered to Connor's side. She sat on the sofa arm to get his attention. It worked.

"It is cold," he repeated.

Ellene lowered her voice. "I know, but she's been so good and cooped up for the past few days. She needs to burn some energy. I'll go out with her."

Connor's eyebrows raised. "You?"

"Me, if I can find something for my feet." She turned toward Aunt Phyllis and raised her voice. "What size are your boots?"

"Mine?"

Ellene nodded. "I'd like to go out with Caitlin for a while."

"They're eights."

"Close enough," Ellene said. "Do you mind?"

"Not at all. Caitlin needs a little fun."

Ellene gave Connor what she hoped was a haughty look. At least she and Aunt Phyllis were on the same page — although that possibility set her on edge.

Caitlin beamed and leaped away from the window to find her boots before bounding up the stairs to her room.

Ellene grasped Conner's aunt's boots and set them in front of her. Since she had been wearing most of his aunt's other clothes, she might as well wear her boots, too, she figured. She slipped one on her foot, then the other, noting they were a bit loose. They would have to do.

Ellene eyed Connor lounging on the sofa, seemingly, without a care in the world. "What are you doing about your job?" she asked.

He glanced at her, punching the TV remote to a new channel. "I called this morning."

"And that's it? They don't care how long you're stranded?"

"They care, but I can't do anything about it, and neither can they."

Connor folded his arms and leaned back, his eyes focused on the television. She saw him sending her an occasional look, but she ignored him.

When Caitlin came down the stairs, she carried her scarf and mittens. Ellene pulled the child's jacket from a hook near the door, and in moments, they were ready.

"Do you have gloves and a scarf?" Aunt Phyllis asked, eyeing her bare head.

"I have leather gloves."

"They won't do," she snorted.

She reached into the arm of her jacket and pulled out a plaid scarf and mittens from her pocket. "Here, and don't get them too wet."

Ellene hid her smile. "I'll take care of them as if they were mine." Although she wondered how a person built a snowman without getting gloves wet.

The terrier stood, nose to the door jamb, waiting to make his escape. Ellene's heart softened. "I'll take the dog out for a while if that's okay."

"Just keep an eye on him," Phyllis said.

"Will do."

The dog bounced at her heels as they stepped into the deepening snow. The ground was slippery beneath, but Ellene drew in a breath of icy air, pleased to see Caitlin's exuberance.

They worked together, rolling a large ball for the bottom of the snowman, then began another when she heard the door open and saw Connor stepping outside, donned in his jacket and gloves.

"Daddy, look what we're doing," Caitlin sang out.

He waved and ambled toward them.

"Couldn't resist the fun?" Ellene asked.

The dog leaped around Connor's feet, and Ellene waited for him to trip again. Instead, Connor sidestepped the animal, bent down and caught his collar. "Time for the chain," he said, tethering the dog. "For his safety."

"Whose safety? I saw you on the ground."

"True," he said, closing the distance between them.

He reached out and caught her coat collar, and before she knew what he'd done, she felt the icy snow slip beneath her sweater.

"You rat," she said, facing him with a

handful of snow from the ball she'd been making. She gave it a toss, but she missed.

While he bent to grab another handful, she charged him with the ball she had hidden and thrust it down his neck. Caitlin joined in, and the snowman-making project turned into a snowball fight.

Connor charged her, wrapped his arms around her body and drew her close, using his fingers to pry open her hands. She breathed hard from the struggle, and when she looked up, his mouth was only inches from hers.

His scent mingled with the crisp air, and she felt her heart skip.

Connor's smile faded while his gaze probed hers. She tried to hide her feelings, but she could tell from his look he'd guessed that the closeness had sent her back in time.

Unaware of their emotional struggle, Caitlin squeezed between them, wriggling and laughing to be part of the fray. Connor lowered his arms and lifted Caitlin into his embrace as if she could provide the barricade to keep their emotions in check.

Why had she allowed this to happen? She'd let down her guard. It was too easy to do that here at the cottage. Too many memories. Too many good times. Too little protection from the past.

Connor wrestled with Caitlin, teasing her with handfuls of snow and dodging her attempts to plop a glob of wet stuff down his jacket.

The terrier's yipping brought Aunt Phyllis to the door, and soon they were back to finishing the forgotten snowman. By the time they'd finished, dusk had settled, and the white snow looked gray and purple in the muted light.

Connor carried Caitlin into the house, and Ellene stood outside a moment, sensing that her determination to stay aloof was sinking as surely as the winter sun.

CHAPTER EIGHT

Ellene rolled over and felt Caitlin's warm body at her side. The little girl had cuddled to her during the night, and Ellene had a difficult time sleeping, not from the closeness but from a maternal longing that smothered her.

Connor had had other sleeping arrangements in mind, but Caitlin had her own. She wanted Ellene to sleep in her bed with her. Connor continued to insist that his aunt use his bed, and though she was set against it, for once Connor had won the battle.

Ellene slipped her feet out of bed and sat up, eyeing the clock. She shifted to move her feet beneath the blankets again, then changed her mind. If she got up early, she might get some work done. Aunt Phyllis's eager conversation had been distracting, although Ellene realized the woman was lonely. She tried to accept the elderly woman's friendly chatter, but the subject was often about relationships and forgiveness and any other topic that seemed to further her matchmaking attempts.

Ellene dressed quietly, slipping into the same black slacks she'd worn the day she arrived, and a borrowed pullover from Connor's aunt, then crept from the room. She tiptoed down the stairs and halted when she saw Connor sitting at the table holding a cup between his hands as if to warm them. Before she could turn and go back upstairs, he saw her.

"Good morning," he said.

"Sofa too short?"

He nodded. "But that wasn't it. I was just restless."

She had been, too, thinking about the snow fight and their embrace that had set her on edge.

"Coffee's fresh," he said, resting his cheek against his fist.

His eyes looked sunken and tired, and she knew he'd probably sat up much of the night. She could easily sleep on the sofa and she would insist tonight if she were still held captive on the island.

"I need to buy some clothes unless the *Bramble* comes to our rescue."

"I called this morning. Doesn't look good.

The weather forecast says we may have a break in another day or so."

Ellene didn't hold stock in weather forecasts. "Then I'll go out later and see if I can find a couple of things."

"I might go into town, too. I'm hoping the coast guard brought in some emergency groceries. We're low on milk, and we should pick up some cereal. When the cold snap breaks, we often lose power."

"Thanks for cheering me up." She filled a cup, then looked at the last heel in the bread bag. "Add bread to that list."

She found an English muffin in the refrigerator and popped it into the toaster, then sat at the table.

Silence hovered over them, each seeming to avoid the other.

Connor stirred. "I'm sorry about yesterday when I grabbed you. It seemed so natural. I wasn't thinking."

"I know."

The conversation died as quickly as it had come alive.

Ellene felt uneasy in the silence. "I'll sleep on the sofa tonight. You look terrible."

"It wasn't the sofa. I'm okay."

She heard the toaster pop and rose to butter her muffin, knowing it wasn't okay. She would insist she sleep on the sofa tonight,

122

but not now. Maybe God would surprise her with an open channel today, despite the weather forecast, and she could go home.

"Can't sleep on that bed." Aunt Phyllis's voice sailed from Connor's bedroom. "I get the sofa. No arguments."

Connor looked at Ellene and grinned. She couldn't help but laugh. Without knowing it, Aunt Phyllis had settled the matter.

"We're going into town, Aunt Phyllis, do you need anything?"

Her face brightened as she looked from Ellene to Connor. "You two are going to town?"

"I have to pick up a few things," Ellene said, not wanting to hurt her feelings, but she was tired of wearing the woman's ill-fitting clothing.

"Groceries," Connor said, almost at the same time Ellene responded.

"Have fun," she said, a wry look curving her lips.

Ellene went upstairs to put herself together with the little makeup she'd carried in her purse. She was weary of washing out her underwear each night and putting it on damp in the morning. The outside chill seemed to penetrate the walls in the bedroom upstairs, and she didn't want to leave her garments hanging downstairs in the bathroom.

When she'd dressed and come down, Connor was standing by the door wearing his jacket. He seemed to be in a hurry, and Ellene wondered why.

"I'll be ready in a minute. I need to find my shoes."

When she bent to look beneath the sofa for them, Caitlin's voice penetrated the silence.

"Where are you going?"

"To town," Connor said. "We'll be back soon."

"I want to go," she said, darting back up the stairs.

Connor looked exasperated, and Ellene realized that he might have hoped to be alone with her. She'd sensed he had things on his mind since the snowball incident. He gave her an irritated look.

"Sorry," she said. "I can't go without my shoes."

While she slipped them on, Caitlin came sailing back down the stairs, dressed in a mismatched getup that made Ellene chuckle.

Connor shook his head. "She could use a few lessons in coordinating color and print." He glanced down at his knit shirt and jeans.

"I'm afraid she has my taste in clothing."

Ellene had never noticed Connor's lack of taste, but then maybe his mother had helped him choose his attire when they were teens.

At the car, Caitlin wanted to join them in the front seat, and to end the problem, Ellene volunteered to ride in back.

"I want to sit with you," Caitlin said, the admiration in her eyes so evident.

Ellene heard Connor's sigh and figured that was what he'd wanted to talk about with her when they were alone. She gave Connor a questioning look, and he only shrugged, so she and Caitlin climbed into the back as if Connor were their chauffeur.

"We're off, James," she said once she had Caitlin buckled into the seat and had hooked her own.

He observed her through the rearview mirror without a response.

In town, Ellene suggested Connor drop her at a clothing store. He parked, and to her surprise, they all climbed out. "You want to go shopping with me?"

"I want to," Caitlin said.

Connor didn't respond.

Ellene gazed at the stores and saw the Riverfront Shop with ladies' clothing displayed in the windows.

Connor touched her arm and pointed.

Across the street, she saw another store, Country Scenes, Ltd. At least she had choices.

Connor opened the door to the Riverfront Shop, and Ellene stepped inside with Caitlin on her heels. He stood close to the door while she wandered through the shop, eyeing the prices and wondering if she could deduct her garments as a business expense.

"I like this," Caitlin said, pulling out a pink sweatshirt with a sad dog on the front and letters beneath which read, No Bone To Pick. She grinned, but pink wasn't her color, and she moved along. Caitlin stayed by the garment for a moment as if willing her to buy it, but she decided she wasn't going to spoil the child by pleasing her every whim.

She checked out a row of knit tops with long sleeves, then checked the slacks. She'd worn her black pair until they were pitiful. She selected a couple of pairs, gathered the other items and headed toward the dressing room.

Before she could close the louvered doors, Caitlin had joined her, watching with big eyes. Ellene slipped on the navy slacks. She could use a new pair. They fit except for the length, and she assumed Connor's aunt had a needle and thread.

Then she studied the tops, a burgundy one with navy edging and one she noticed Caitlin eyeing, a navy-and-pink stripe.

"I like this one," Caitlin said, fingering the fabric of the striped top.

The child loved pink, and Caitlin slipped it over her head, watching the child's observant face change to a grin. "You look beautiful."

Ellene's heart skipped, and she stooped to hug the little girl. Beautiful. She doubted if anyone had called her that before. "Thank you, Caitlin. That's the sweetest thing anyone has ever said."

The child's grin grew. "Are you going to buy it?"

"I have to, don't I? Who could pass up something that makes her beautiful?"

She redressed and headed for the checkout counter, but as she did, she noticed a display of children's sweatshirts. She paused, checking out the pink ones. Caitlin adhered to her side, not saying anything, but Ellene knew the child's silent wish. She spotted one with a puppy on the front. Everyone Loves Me it said beneath the fluffy dog.

Ellene waved toward Connor, and he stepped closer. "Does she wear a six?"

He nodded. "But you don't have to —"

"I want to," she said.

He gave a one-shoulder shrug and returned to the exit.

After selecting Caitlin's shirt, she strode toward the checkout but paused when she spotted the rack where Caitlin had admired the sweatshirt for her. She found her size and pulled it from the hanger. Could it hurt to spoil the child a little? What was wrong with agreeing and buying herself a shirt?

Ellene held up the two shirts. "Now we'll be twins," she said, watching Caitlin's smile glow brighter than the sun on the snow.

After picking up a few smaller items, the clerk rang up her bill, and Ellene paid with a credit card. She'd found most of what she needed.

"You're spoiling her," Connor whispered as they left the shop.

"Girls are meant to be spoiled."

"Really," he said and gave her a look that sent her pulse on a trot. "I'll keep that in mind.

Connor spread out on the sofa, watching Ellene at her computer wearing the pink sweatshirt with the dog on the front she'd bought while shopping on Tuesday.

Ellene had wended her way into Caitlin's heart, and Connor didn't know what to do about it. It seemed too late now to stop it. The hurt would happen when Ellene trotted home without looking back.

He knew Ellene had a soft heart. Buying the sweatshirt was an example, but in another moment, he had watched her back stiffen and her tone change from the normal woman he knew to the business woman he'd recently come to know. He didn't like the bumpy ride.

Two more days had passed, and now, Thursday, they'd been holed up for five days. Today, as usual, Caitlin sat close to Ellene, wearing her pink shirt.She shifted between working at her drawings and watching Ellene beside her. The vision seared into Connor's brain. Good or bad? He feared for his daughter's happiness.

"Caitlin, it's time for bed," Connor said.

She gave him an unhappy look, but folded the cover of her drawing book and slid from the chair. She headed toward him with an argument in her eyes. "But Daddy —"

He held up his hand to stop her. "You had a fun day. We played games, and now we all need to rest. We'll have more fun tomorrow."

She leaned against him, tucking her head against his chest while her gaze settled on

Ellene. "But I don't want to go to bed alone."

Ellene looked up, but before she could react, Aunt Phyllis offered a solution. "I'll go up and lie down with you, Caitlin. I'm tired tonight."

From her look, Connor knew that wasn't the result Caitlin wanted, but she had enough good sense to accept the offer. She headed for the stairs with Pepper bounding at her heels. Aunt Phyllis gave Connor a knowing smile and joined them on the stairs.

Relief washed over Connor. He'd longed for time to talk with Ellene alone, and the time had never seemed to happen. He'd thought on Tuesday when they'd gone shopping he might have a minute to discuss a few things, but Caitlin had put an end to that.

Ellene refocused on the computer, but as their footsteps faded up the stairs, she stopped and rubbed her eyes.

"How about taking a break?" he asked, hoisting himself to a sitting position.

She massaged the back of her neck. "That's probably a good idea. I'm having a difficult time concentrating."

So was he.

Connor eyed the TV remote, but hesitated

when he saw her snap the lid closed on the computer. He felt hopeful, realizing she had decided to stop working for the evening.

After listening to Aunt Phyllis's Bible verses for the past three days they'd spent under the same roof, they'd begun to sink in. He'd gone to Sunday school as a child, but in his teen years, he'd slipped away from church, and his faith had become as dormant as his morals.

When he thought about that recently, he guessed that trying to explain his moral failures was easier when he didn't profess his love for the Lord. But truth didn't hide for long, and he was pleased that his aunt's influence had nurtured Caitlin. He'd heard her singing a child's hymn that Aunt Phyllis must have taught her.

He'd wanted to tell Ellene that, in part, his failure to fight for her love had been based on his failure as a Christian. But that was the easy answer. It had been more complex.

When he looked up, Ellene still sat by the closed computer until she finally rose and ambled across the room, a mixture of beauty and comedy in his aunt's huge fuzzy slippers.

Ellene must have noticed him looking. She plopped into the chair nearby and lifted one foot. "I know. I look like a clown."

"But a lovely one," he said. Watching the expression on her face, he wished he hadn't been so candid.

They sat in silence, dealing with their own thoughts. Her eyes lifted for a moment, then lowered to her lap.

"Caitlin is smitten," he said.

It took her a minute to lift her head. "I know. I'm concerned."

"So am I, but I don't know what to do about it."

"Neither do I." She rubbed her temple. "I didn't ask to be stranded here, Connor. My intention was to see the cottage, make my notes and leave."

"I know." Yet he wanted to ask if she hadn't found some warm moments here. "You've handled this very well."

"I had little choice," she said.

Her gaze caught his, and he saw her gaze dart away then return. "I don't mean it hasn't been nice at times."

He felt as if the floor dropped from beneath his feet and took his breath away.

"Caitlin is a joy, and your aunt has given me some good laughs and some spiritual wisdom. She's made me think."

"Is that why you pull away from me, Ellene? Because of spiritual wisdom?"

She looked as if she didn't understand.

"I've changed. I'm more solid in my relationship with the Lord, but it was a long struggle. When I married Melissa, she and I agreed Caitlin should have a chance to know the Lord. We began attending church." He drew in a deep breath, remembering. "I was on the verge of giving my life to Christ, but when Melissa died, so did my faith. How was I supposed to raise a child alone, a child I didn't wan—" He caught himself. "A child I didn't know how to care for like a mother would."

She drew back as if she'd put the ending on his cut-off sentence. "I'm sorry, Connor. Even Christians don't always know why things happen."

"But I want to know about you. Is that why you distanced yourself from me, because you don't think I have faith?"

She looked surprised. "I suppose it's instinctive to pull away. It's not easy to forget how much you hurt me."

"And you hurt me." His stomach twisted as the words left his mouth.

"I suppose I did." Her eyes misted. "Let me be honest." She paused, and he saw her swallow as if trying to control her emotions. "I had a great scenario planned, Connor."

Scenario? "What do you mean? What did

you do, write a script?"

"I thought I'd send you off, and you'd be angry. Then you'd think about us and our relationship, and you'd be devastated. You'd realize how much I meant to you, and you'd come back and plead with me to take you back, and —"

"You what?" He lifted his hand as if trying to grasp her meaning. "I can't believe this. Why did you send me away then? Why did you return the ring?"

"Because I thought you'd come back and ask me to forgive you, and I would have."

Was he the one to be forgiven? His hand shook as he lowered it back to the sofa arm. "If you played that lightly with our relationship, Ellene, it was right for it to end. Marriage is for better or worse. No marriage is perfect. No relationship is perfect. It takes work."

She didn't say a word but kept her head lowered.

"Do you remember Aunt Phyllis going on the other day about how two are better than one? I don't know how she worked it into the conversation, but she's a born matchmaker, and she was reminding us, I think, that God meant people to be in twos."

"I remember. How could I forget?"

"That verse has stuck with me. Two are

better than one because when one falls the other picks him up, and when they go to bed, two will stay warmer than one."

She held up her hand. "I know, Connor, and if an enemy attacks them, two can defend themselves. 'A cord of three strands is not quickly broken.' I know that."

"Can you picture the strength of those cords? A man, a woman and God. That's what we were lacking back then. You had faith. I didn't."

Her expression changed from frustration to question.

"Your parents always welcomed me into your home as a friend of yours. But once we were engaged, I always figured your father was disappointed that we had decided to get married."

A frown appeared, and she shook her head. "That's not true."

"But I thought it was. Your father had always been kind to me. He was when I called about this job. He's a man who lives by God's commandments so he does the best he can not to judge, but he knows what the Bible says. A Christian man or woman should not consider marriage to someone who's not a believer."

"You are a believer."

"A very weak one then. I'm stronger now,

because of what I've gone through."

"Are you telling me that's why you didn't come back and try again?"

How could he answer her question and not lie? "At the time, that was my biggest fear. The other problem was your dad owned a business. Mine was a blue-collar worker — dirty fingernails, grungy clothes. We didn't have dinner parties and a house full of chattering relatives."

"That didn't mean a thing. My dad owns a construction company. He learned from the ground up. Our family doesn't judge others by where they work or how much money they have."

"But your father wanted the best for you, just like I want the best for Caitlin. The thought didn't cross my mind until we became engaged. We were young and in love. When I started college, I realized the difference between the rich and the poor."

"So if I'd been poor, you would have loved me more?"

"No. I couldn't have loved you more."

She looked away as if disgusted with his response, but she hadn't understood him. He'd loved her as much as any man could at his age, and that's why he'd fallen apart when she gave him back the ring.

Ellene had put on her business face again,

but Connor wasn't going to stop now. He deserved time for his unanswered questions. "What about you, Ellene? If you loved me so much, if you wanted us to be married, why did you play games with our relationship?"

"It wasn't a game. I was confused. I was young and was looking for a fairy-tale relationship. I didn't want you to spend time with your buddies or tell me you had a club meeting on campus."

"That's not realistic."

"I realize that now. Back then I was —"

"Spoiled . . . like Caitlin."

He could tell she didn't want to hear that by the look on her face, but it was true.

"I was naive."

"You were spoiled." They'd both been naive.

Ellene's eyes narrowed and she rose. "When I come out of the bathroom, I don't want to lay eyes on you, Connor. Good night."

She spun around, marched into the bathroom and slammed the door.

Connor's eyes rang with her dismissal. He sat there a moment, willing the door to open so they could finish what they'd started. As he stared at the barricade between them, his hope vanished and he felt empty. This wasn't how he'd wanted the conversation to end.

CHAPTER NINE

Ellene waited in the bathroom until she heard Connor close the door of his bedroom. She peeked out and saw the nightlight turned on in the hallway and knew he'd gone to bed.

She opened the door and tiptoed out into the living room. The house was quiet, and she assumed Aunt Phyllis had fallen asleep with Caitlin. She saw no point in waking the woman to traipse down to the sofa.

After finding the pile of bed linens in a chest under the window, she made up the sofa and settled down. Though her body lay still, her mind continued to struggle with her conversation with Connor. She'd been wrong, and she knew it, but it was too late now.

His faith journey filled her thoughts. She'd never let that stop her from loving Connor. He had every admirable trait that the scriptures commanded — kindness, gentleness, compassion, humility and forgiveness.

Forgiveness. She needed to find forgiveness in her heart. Connor had walked away because she'd sent him, and he'd explained what he'd been thinking. Nothing made sense to her, and now so much time had passed since they'd been in love. Ellene thought she'd been over the breakup for a long time. Apparently she hadn't been.

Guilt shrouded Ellene's thoughts when those memories led her down an unwanted path. She'd tried to forget another part of her life, but it always came back to haunt her. After she'd heard Connor had married so soon after their ended engagement, she'd dated any man who asked, but the relationships felt empty and sad. Yet at the time, she'd been so fixated on hurting Connor that she didn't care.

Finally, she'd stopped, determined to remain true to herself, remembering how useless it felt and knowing what God expected from Christian relationships.

Yet she recalled the day she'd met Owen. He'd captured her interest, and after months of dating, he'd tempted her emotions. They'd talked about marriage, and Ellene relived the day they'd looked at rings. With the promise of marriage, he'd convinced her to show her love. She'd given in, and before the wedding date was finalized, he'd walked away, too.

Afterward, Ellene felt dirty, unloved and unforgiven. She'd gained nothing. She'd allowed emotions to rule her heart instead of her head. From that day, she'd promised God never again to give herself to anyone outside of marriage. The guilt and sorrow, the chance of disease or pregnancy was not worth it.

Now she thought about Connor. He stirred her. She cared about him, but she realized their past left her feeling uncertain and untrusting. They'd both changed, but she had no guarantee things would be any better the second time.

The one thing that stayed in her mind was that Connor had always been moral. He'd never touched her. He'd wanted to, but he'd respected her Christian upbringing, and he'd promised never to allow passion to overrule what was right and good. She would always admire him for his respect and protection.

Ellene pressed her eyes closed, wishing sleep would come. The wind made night sounds, and she heard the creak of rafters and the crack of branches breaking from the weight of ice. The night-light gave her assurance the electricity hadn't failed them.

Morning arrived with the sound of Connor's footsteps approaching her. She pulled down the blanket and opened her eyes. "Up early?"

"I didn't sleep well," he said, passing by and heading for the kitchen. "Why did you sleep here?"

"It didn't make sense to wake your aunt." She pushed herself up using the arm of the sofa and braced her back with her free hand. The sofa wasn't the most comfortable place to sleep, but she felt good that she'd taken a turn.

When she lowered her feet, they felt cold against the parquet floor. "I suggest you add carpet to this area when you do your renovations. I think it would help hold the heat better."

He grunted something, and she leaned back, covering her gown with the blanket and watched him. While he faced the counter, she decided to escape to change her clothes. She darted into the bathroom, hopped into the warm shower, then slipped into her clothing.

When she came out, dressed again in her pink sweatshirt that said No Bone To Pick, the scent of coffee filled the great room. Finally feeling at home, she ambled across the room, pulled out a cup and poured.

142

She leaned her back against the counter while Connor had his head stuck inside the refrigerator. "I'm sorry about last night," she said.

He jerked his head out so fast, it hit the edge of the freezer door. Rubbing the spot, he turned to stare at her. "That would have been nice to hear before I went to bed."

Ellene was almost sorry she'd apologized, but she tried to put herself in Connor's shoes. He'd been candid and honest. She'd offered little to the discussion. "You're right. I make bad choices."

He looked at her a moment, then stuck out his hand. "Truce?"

She gazed at his strong fingers pointed toward her and clasped his hand. "Truce," she agreed.

They didn't say much more, and she curled up on the sofa thinking about her job and her home while listening to Connor bang around in the kitchen. Though the cottage had begun to grow on her in the past days, she continued to wonder about living on the island full-time. What about employment?

She glanced his way, and when he swung around, she voiced her concern. "Why not keep the cottage for summer? Caitlin will still enjoy its charm, but during a more seasonable time of year."

He wandered over and sat on the sofa arm. "I'd like to own a business, and I can't do it owning two houses. This one doesn't have as much value as my house in St. Clair Shores. I'm getting a good price for it —"

"You mean it's sold?"

"It will be when the buyers' mortgage is approved, and that should be any day. Then with my inheritance, I can take a chance on buying a business."

The news left her uneasy. If he'd sold his house, he couldn't turn back now. "What kind of business?"

"I'm a salesman. I've been looking around."

She sensed he was being evasive, and she decided not to push him, but that added to her concern. Why wouldn't he tell her what business?

"It's not my pride, either, if that's what you're thinking. I want a job with regular hours. If I'm the owner I have control. I want a business that's more child-friendly."

"Child-friendly? Are you buying a toy store?"

He looked irked. "No, I mean a shop where I have an office. Can you picture a kid hanging around a car showroom?"

She couldn't but that wasn't the point.

144

"It's your money, Connor. I have no say-so, but you know new businesses take a few years to catch on and most fail. You need a lot of financial backing."

He rose and walked away. "Thanks for your vote of confidence."

"I didn't mean it like that, Connor. I only meant —"

"A gentle answer turns away wrath, but a harsh word stirs up anger."

Ellene spun around when she heard Aunt Phyllis's voice project from the doorway near the stairs. "Sorry, I couldn't help overhearing you argue."

"We're not arguing," Connor said.

"You aren't snuggling like two bugs in a rug, either."

Ellene chuckled, and so did Connor.

Aunt Phyllis gave them both a look as she headed for the telephone. She picked up the receiver and hit the speed dial. "I'm checking on the ferry," she said into the phone.

Ellene listened, anxious for the response.

"You don't say," Aunt Phyllis said, glancing her way.

Ellene perked up. She wasn't sure what that meant, but it sounded hopeful. When Phyllis hung up the phone, Ellene waited for the news.

"Temperatures are warmer today and tomorrow. That could mean a breakthrough."

"Finally," Ellene said. Being with Connor had become impossible. She longed to let her heart rule. She adored Caitlin, and she ached for the little girl, but trust seemed so impossible, even if she did forgive Connor.

Breakfast was quiet until Caitlin came down the stairs with Pepper. She opened the door, and the dog darted outside as usual.

Connor jumped up. "Why did you open the door?" he yelled, then darted outside after the dog.

Caitlin stood inside, her lip sticking out an inch.

In a moment, Connor reappeared with the dog in his arms. "You can't open the door like that, Caitlin. Pepper runs out. You know that."

"I'm sorry." Her lip trembled. "I wanted to see if it was warm so we could all go out and play."

Ellene's chest tightened. The child had been housebound for the past couple of days, and she'd been so good. "We can go for a walk later, Caitlin."

"Can we build a snowman again?"

"It's a little warm today. It'll be too slushy."

"I have a sled in the back shed," Aunt Phyllis said.

Ellene caught Caitlin's attention and clapped her hands. "That'll be fun."

She looked at Connor, who seemed to be irritable, and she was sure it was what she'd said to him about his business idea. He hadn't asked for her opinion, and she needed to keep her mouth shut until he did.

They returned to breakfast, and before she took a bite, Ellene heard her cell phone ring. She rose and pulled it from her handbag. Her father's voice shot from the earpiece. "Are you ever coming home?" he blurted.

"I'd love to, Dad. We're still stranded."

"Living on an island is hogwash. We have customers who are crabbing about their appointments, and we don't know what to say."

"I don't, either." She carried the phone toward the bathroom, went inside and shut the door. "Look, Dad, I'm ready to come home. Even if I hire a helicopter or plane to fly me home, my car's still on the island. Can you be patient another day? It looks like the weather is breaking."

"That's the last time we'll do business on

Harsens Island," he said.

"I told you —"

"Sorry, Ellene. It's not the island. It's your clients' complaining. Call the Dartmouths, would you? And the Cabonis."

"I will, Dad. I'm sorry."

"Not your fault. Give Connor my best wishes. Don't tell him what I said. The boy can't help that the cottage is on the island."

The boy. She shook her head. Connor was a man, a tall, broad-shouldered, good-looking man, and that's what was killing her. "I'll send your best wishes, Daddy. Be patient a little while, and I'll make those calls."

"Love you."

"Love you, Daddy."

"Ellene."

"Yes."

"Call your mother. She's driving me crazy, too."

She said she would and hung up, grinning at her parents' inability to comprehend she was an independent woman who didn't need to be looked after.

"Trouble on the home front?" Connor asked when she left the bathroom.

"Clients," she said. "They miss me."

"I can understand that," he said.

148

"I'll miss you if you go," Caitlin added.

Ellene's chest tightened. "I'll miss you, too."

Caitlin moaned to Connor, disappointed that Ellene had to work, but he convinced her they would sled after dinner.

Connor knew that time dragged for Caitlin, so he kept his promise. When the meal had ended, his aunt said she'd clean the kitchen, and they headed outside.

The temperatures had cooled from earlier in the day. Connor settled Caitlin on the sled and noticed the trees and lines were coated with ice, and the ground had frozen into deeper ruts.

He felt the strain of his muscles as he tugged the sled across the ground while Caitlin giggled. Ellene jogged beside him, and he felt more lighthearted than he had all day.

"Let Ellene ride with me, Daddy," Caitlin called.

He eyed the trim woman by his side and gave a nod. "Hop on."

"You're kidding."

"Afraid?"

"No, but I think you'll kill yourself."

Caitlin rose, and Ellene settled on the sled, trying to hold her feet above the ground. Then Caitlin sat between her legs. "Mush!" she called and cracked an imaginary whip.

Connor dug his feet into the rutted ground, his legs tensing as he picked up speed. He felt the burn in his muscles, and he figured if nothing more, he'd get some good exercise.

Ellene's laughter joined Caitlin's, and Connor felt as if life couldn't get better, but as soon as the thought entered his mind, it faded. Tomorrow or the next day, Ellene would walk out the door.

"Run faster, Daddy," Caitlin called.

Pepper came bounding out of nowhere and leaped at Connor's heels. He lost his footing, skidded to the ground and the sled took a ninety-degree turn, then tipped over.

"Are you okay?" Connor called, seeing Ellene and Caitlin in a jumble.

Ellene raised on one elbow and grinned, watching him hoist himself from the ground while Pepper jumped around him.

"Get out of my way, Pepper," he said, scooting around the dog to reach Caitlin and Ellene. "You're okay?"

"We're fine," Ellene said, pulling her leg from beneath the sled. "At least, I think so."

"You look fine to me," he said.

He helped her up, and once again, the

closeness riffled her senses. "Thanks. I think I've had enough sledding."

"Not me," Caitlin said.

They laughed, righted the sled, set Caitlin back on with Pepper locked between her legs and headed back toward the house.

The sun hung low in the sky, turning the snow to a grayish hue, and the last rays glinted on the ice-coated trees and power lines. An icicle dropped from a tree as they walked past, knifing into the crusted snow.

"Can't you keep up?" Connor asked Ellene as she lagged behind.

"It's getting slipperier."

"It's freezing again," he said, reaching back to grab her hand.

She laughed as he forced her to trot alongside him. He loved the sound of her laughter and the feel of her hand in his. He'd warned himself not to let his emotions get carried away, but he hadn't listened to himself, and Caitlin hadn't helped the situation at all with her obvious admiration of Ellene.

When they arrived home, Connor leaned the sled against the house and shooed the dog in first. The room's warmth blanketed them, and he realized his cheeks were stinging from the cold and wind.

"Have fun?" Aunt Phyllis asked.

151

"We did until Pepper entered the scene."

She shrugged. "I opened the door and he vamoosed."

"I had fun," Caitlin said, pulling off her boots and dropping them by the door. She gave a large yawn.

"Tired," Connor said, giving her a hug as he passed. He looked at his aunt. "The wires don't look good."

"I saw ice on the trees," she said. "We probably should prepare, just in case."

Ellene plopped on the sofa. "You two sound like doom and gloom."

"Being realistic," Connor said. With that thought in mind, he located a couple of flashlights and set out two candleholders.

Caitlin had curled up on the sofa and rested her cheek against the arm. Connor glanced her way and watched her deep breathing. "She's out already."

Her eyes popped open. "No, I'm not. I'm resting like you do, Daddy."

Connor smiled, recalling a few times he'd drifted off on the sofa and given her that excuse.

"Let's play Old Maid," she said, bolting up from her resting spot.

"I don't think so. It's getting late."

"Just one game?"

Her plaintive voice filtered through his attitude. "What do you say?" He looked at Ellene and his aunt.

Ellene shrugged. "I haven't played Old Maid in years."

"I'll teach you," Caitlin said.

Connor gave Ellene a wink.

Aunt Phyllis found the game, and they sat around the table, matching Little Bo-Peeps and Little Boy Blues.

Caitlin giggled when Connor became the Old Maid, and they agreed to play another game. By the time they'd finished four games, everyone had been the Old Maid except Ellene.

"I'm already an old maid," Ellene said, although Caitlin missed the point, but Connor didn't.

Aunt Phyllis narrowed her eyes. "It's your choice, you know." She followed her comment with a yawn and offered to put Caitlin to bed. She grabbed a flashlight to be safe and headed for the stairs. "Now, you call me when you're ready for bed, Ellene."

Ellene gave her a wink, then picked up the cards and put them away.

Connor moved to the fireplace and crouched. They hadn't enjoyed a fire in a few days, and tonight seemed like a perfect time. He stacked kindling on the bottom, tucked in a fire starter and lit a match. The wax and sawdust starter blazed and soon the kindling began to crackle. He waited until the flames rose, then threw on a small log.

Rising, he stretched his back. "I think that fall did more damage than I thought. I'm stiff."

"It was fun," Ellene said, curling her feet beneath her as she gazed at the fire.

Connor's stomach tightened, seeing the flickering glow reflect on her upturned face. A warm smile curved her mouth.

"It was," he said, joining her on the sofa. He stayed closer to the far end, not wanting to cause her concern.

As he leaned against the cushion, the kitchen light flickered and went out. Connor gave a soft chuckle as the fire's glow filled the room.

"I think you made this happen with your pessimism," Ellene said.

"I call it wisdom."

"You do?" She shook her head.

Connor rose and snapped off the lights and pulled cords on the appliances. "Safer to do this than have a power surge."

He returned and sat closer, turning to face her. "It'll be cold tonight. You'll need extra blankets."

"I'll sleep down here by the fire. I'll be fine."

He didn't open his mouth, afraid he'd say something that he'd be sorry for. "With the weather warming, I'd guess the ferry will open soon — if not tomorrow, then the next day."

"Then I can go home." Her voice sounded soft and uncertain.

"That's good news for you."

She rested her neck against the cushion. "Yes, but I'll . . ." She lifted her head and shook it.

"You like not having to get up for work."

"That's nice, but —"

"What is it?"

"It's Caitlin. She's a beautiful child, Connor. I know how attached she is, and I feel responsible. She's grown on me, too. I'll miss her."

He shifted closer, letting his arm rest on the sofa back. "Ellene, we don't have to be strangers. We've spent nearly a week together — in forced proximity, but it hasn't been too bad, has it?"

She lowered her head, her finger plucking at a loose thread in the sofa fabric. "It's been fine." She lifted her gaze. "Most of the time."

Connor laughed and touched her hand.

"It seemed good to be together again, even for business."

Ellene didn't respond.

"Speaking of business, if you're still here tomorrow, I'd like your opinion on my business venture."

She arched an eyebrow. "My opinion? Are you sure?"

"I am. I respect your intelligence and business sense. There's a place in town I've been thinking about buying. A sports shop."

"On the island?" She uncurled her legs and slid her feet to the floor. "What about the electricity? They'll probably be closed."

"It's in town, and I'm guessing they still have power there. I'll check in the morning."

"Why is the owner selling the business?"

"He wants off the island, I think." He looked at the expression on her face and knew what she was thinking. "And you don't blame him, I know."

She shrugged. "I don't know about a business on an island. You have limited customers."

"The island has tourists in the summer. I'd just like you to take a look."

"And you want me to be truthful?"

He saw the look on her face and didn't answer. She'd already made up her mind.

CHAPTER TEN

Ellene stepped from Connor's SUV, and a chill skittered down her back. She'd only drunk orange juice this morning, since the electricity hadn't come back on. She would enjoy a hot cup of coffee, especially after learning the town still had power.

"It's colder than predicted," Connor said, closing the SUV's door. He swung his hand toward the shop in front of them. "This is it."

Ellene gazed at the sign. Island Sports Shop. She studied the street-front windows with their unimaginative design. She glanced at golf clubs, polo shirts, tennis rackets and badminton sets, all seemingly dumped into the window display.

Connor pushed open the door and motioned her inside. She stood a moment within the threshold, noting no customers browsing inside the store. She wandered down the first aisle, then the second, viewing golf shoes, tennis shoes, archery sets and fishing gear.

She also noticed dust everywhere. The shop needed a good cleaning. Signs of neglect gave her an uneasy feeling. No pride in the business, no customers, no success.

Her mind spun with curiosity. On a small island, how much business would a sports shop have?

As they neared the counter, the clerk was watching them. "Can I help you?"

"We're just looking," Connor said. He paused in front of the register. "Mr. Long's not in today?" He turned to Ellene. "He's the owner."

"Mr. Long lives off the island in the winter. He couldn't get here without the ferry service."

"Isn't that unusual to live away from your business?" Ellene asked, thinking that hiring help in a sport shop in winter didn't make good business sense.

"He has a full-time job on the mainland."

"Aah," Ellene said, weighing the information and noting Connor hadn't reacted to the statement.

He grasped her arm and steered her away from the counter to peruse the rest of the shop. The contents seemed much the same — baseball bats and mitts, basketballs and hoops — nothing for the winter months.

"I've seen enough, I think," she said, edging toward the doorway. "How about finding a restaurant so we can have a cup of coffee?"

"That sounds good," he said as he pushed open the door and they stepped outside. "So, what do you think?"

"You want me to be honest."

He nodded, his eyes searching hers.

"I think you'd be throwing your money away."

He pulled himself to full height. "I figured you'd say that."

"You asked and now you don't trust my opinion?"

"It's not that. I saw it on your face yesterday when I asked you to take a look."

Her shoulders tightened. "You're wrong, and if you'd have really asked questions and looked at the shop, then you'd understand why I say this."

He pursed his lips and shoved his hands into his pockets. "You don't have a lot of faith in me, do you?"

"It has nothing to do with faith in you. It's about having no faith in a business that's dead."

He reached for her arm to help her over a slippery stretch of sidewalk, and her reflex caused her to pull away. From his expression, Ellene knew she'd hurt his feelings.

"I don't want to argue about this, Connor. I just hate to see you throw away your money on a bad business decision."

He was quiet a moment, hunched over, she assumed against the cold, then he turned his head toward her. "Why do you assume the business is dead?"

"Do you see any customers?" She scanned the surrounding shops. "Look over there." She pointed across the street. "Nick's Hardware. You went there Monday for supplies, and there, Gale's Hair Salon. Over there's the Island Video. You see the cars?" She swung her hand toward the space in front of the sport shop. "Do you see any here except yours?"

He shook his head and unlocked the car door, then opened it for her, the hot coffee forgotten.

She slid inside, sorry that she'd been so blunt, but she couldn't see Connor taking his inheritance and sinking it into a failing business, which is what she guessed the store would be.

Connor slid in, turned the key in the ignition and pulled away. He didn't speak, and Ellene knew he was upset.

She opened her mouth to apologize, but

the damage had already been done. Instead she looked out the passenger window, asking herself what she should have said. She could have lied, but she'd never forgive herself if he bought the store and lost his money.

Connor snapped on the radio, turning the volume so loud they couldn't talk if they wanted to. He kept his eyes focused on the road, but when they passed the ferry landing, he slowed, then picked up speed.

Ellene noticed the sign still said Closed and figured he would be glad to get rid of her. Although she tried to pretend it didn't matter, the idea that he wanted to see her leave stung. She leaned her head against the cold glass, thinking about how things could have gone.

She was reminded of her telephone call to her mother: "We'd love to see Connor," she'd said.

Ellene had tried to temper the conversation, but her mother returned to the topic.

"Your birthday's in a couple of weeks. We're having your dinner party here. Why not invite Connor?"

"Let's not get carried away, Mom. We're together on a business deal, nothing more."

"Then there's no harm in inviting him."

Ellene had struggled to get off the telephone and assure her mother she'd be home soon.

Soon. She hoped tomorrow, but despite her declaration to her mother that it was business only between her and Connor, the thought of leaving the island — leaving Caitlin and him — gave her a lonely feeling.

She lifted her forehead from the cold windowpane. "Connor, maybe I jumped to conclusions. I'm sorry."

He looked her way with a shrug. "It doesn't matter."

"It does. I shouldn't have said what I did."

He turned off the radio. "I realize you grew up with a father who has a successful business. I don't know if he ever had to struggle, but since I've known you, your family has been well-off. I'd like to do that for my daughter."

"Connor, I'm not comparing you to —"

"I know it will take time to get the business going. I hope to have enough money to live on, and I'll give this more thought, but if I live on the island, I think it would be nice to work here, too."

"It would, and I'm not comparing you to my father."

"Good, because I'm not him."

She knew that, and in some ways, she was glad. She loved her father, but he had attributes that got on her nerves, too.

One of Aunt Phyllis's Bible verses came to mind. "Be humble and gentle; be patient, bearing with one another in love." Ellene could still hear his aunt's lecture about how relationships are made up of people with differing opinions, and arguments keep a person on his toes and teach patience.

Ellene had to admit she'd been on her toes a lot while being stranded on the island, but without wanting to, she'd found pleasure in it.

"Lights came on while you were gone," Aunt Phyllis said when they arrived back, "and the *Bramble* is heading toward the channel, I hear."

"Then I'll be leaving soon," Ellene said.

"No," Caitlin said. "You can't go home. We'll miss you."

"Remember what I said? I'll miss you, too."

"You'll see each other again," Aunt Phyllis said. "Ellene and your daddy both have to go to work, and you have to go back to school."

"I don't want to go to school."

Connor knelt beside Caitlin and tilted her chin. "So you like this house after all."

She turned her head away. "I like it when

Ellene is here. She plays with me."

"Your Daddy plays with you, too," Ellene said.

She looked at the floor. "But it's more fun when it's all of us."

Connor's heart ached for his daughter. He drew her into his arms and hugged her so tightly he feared he might hurt her. He eased back and looked into her sad eyes. "We'll see Ellene again. She's going to help us fix this cottage into a real house."

She studied Connor's face, then turned to look into Ellene's eyes. "Will I see you again?"

"I'm positive."

"Promise?"

Connor knew a promise had to be real. He turned to Ellene, asking with his eyes and knowing she understood from her expression.

"Promise," she said.

Caitlin wriggled from his arms and gave Ellene a hug.

His mind wavered. Ellene could make him so angry as she did today when she denigrated his ability to make the sports shop a success. She'd hurt his pride. Yet often she filled him with pleasure — her quick mind, the laughter, the tender moments, the years they'd shared.

He watched Caitlin's face. She'd latched onto Ellene as if she were her favorite playmate, and now the ferry service would soon be back in use. Even though Ellene had promised, things would never be the same.

He cared about Ellene more than he could say. Why play with the truth? He'd fallen in love with her again, as irritating as she could be, and it wasn't for Caitlin's sake, either, but for his own. The love he'd felt for Ellene so long ago had only slipped into a compartment in his mind and had been set free since she'd reappeared. He'd lost control of his heart.

Aunt Phyllis broke the silence. "I'm going to run next door for a few things." She slipped on her coat and headed for the door.

"Can I play outside, Daddy? Just for a little while?"

He glanced at Ellene as if to ask for approval for some reason, but she didn't notice. "For a few minutes, but be careful," he said finally.

Caitlin found her coat and boots, then opened the door and bounded outside into the cold air.

Connor stood in silence with Ellene beside him. He had too much to say and so little time. He'd tried to work slowly, letting her

165

know he cherished their friendship. He wanted to tell her he cherished her, but he sensed she was still guarded, and he knew he should move slowly.

"You know," he said, easing his back against the kitchen counter, "this ferry closing has had some effects for me."

She eyed him questioningly.

He grinned. "Aunt Phyllis and her scripture lessons. They've been thrust upon me with a vengeance."

She seemed to weigh what he'd said and then realized he'd been joking. "She has a unique personality."

"She's taught me a lot about faith while we've been cooped up here together. She's a walking Bible. When you're not around, she barrages me with verses on trust and forgiveness."

Ellene finally laughed. "Join the club." She tapped her chest. "She's done the same to me." She looked uneasy a moment and looked away, but when she redirected her focus, she grinned into his eyes. "She's determined you and I should be friends."

"I know." He drew in a lengthy breath, a question clinging to his lips. "What do you think?"

She pursed her lips. "We have a truce."

"Right, but how about more than that?

How about a real friendship?"

"It's possible, I suppose." Her gaze wandered as if in thought. "With time and TLC."

Tender loving care. "I can do that."

She smiled. "Let's see how it goes."

"I can handle that," he said, thrilled to have taken a step forward with her.

"Good." she chuckled and headed toward the back door. She gazed out the window. "Caitlin looks lonely. I think I'll go outside."

"She'll like that." A sweet sensation squeezed Connor's chest. Ellene could be so thoughtful, so loving when she let down her guard, and their candid talk gave him hope for even better things.

Ellene headed across the room, picked up her jacket, then strode to the door. She gave a wave and stepped outside.

Connor stood in the window a moment, his heart in this throat. Ellene would be a wonderful mother to Caitlin — a wonderful mother to her own children. Despite her reservations, she'd succumbed to Caitlin's charm. He realized she didn't know much about kids, but then, neither did he. He'd done the best he could — sometimes frustrated, but always blessed.

He watched Caitlin running across the slippery snow to meet Ellene. He could tell

167

from Caitlin's motions she wanted to make another snowman, but the snow was too wet.

Connor's gaze drifted to the slippery street. The sun had sent down its warming beams onto the earth, and the ice had finally begun to melt. He heard the steady plop of icicles dropping from nearby trees and the eaves of the house.

He turned his attention back to Caitlin as she ran in a wide circle with Ellene pretending she was trying to catch her. He walked away from the window and slipped on his jacket. Why was he inside when the two women he loved were outdoors?

When Connor pulled open the door, Pepper darted between his legs and bounded outside. "Pepper. Get back here," he called as Ellene clapped her hands to draw the dog toward her.

But Caitlin saw Pepper and a smile lit her face. She grabbed a broken tree limb from the ground and tossed the stick. Pepper grabbed it and headed away from them toward the street.

Connor's gaze followed the dog, and his heart stood still when he saw a car veering down the street, its wheels sliding on the icy road. He spotted Caitlin running toward the terrier. He jerked on the doorknob, flung the door wider and saw Ellene dashing toward Caitlin who seemed unaware that a car was charging toward her and Pepper.

"Caitlin," Ellene screamed.

Caitlin glanced over her shoulder and laughed, as if she thought Ellene's call was part of the game.

"Caitlin. Stop!" Connor was running hard with Ellene racing ahead of him.

Pepper darted to the edge of the street, obviously trying to brake, but the ice kept the dog's momentum moving forward.

Connor's heart thundered as Caitlin, who must have spotted the car, lurched forward to grab the dog, but Ellene had reached her and pushed her aside. Caitlin slipped to the ground, but Pepper didn't have a chance to escape. The car skidded sideways and clipped the dog.

Caitlin's scream pierced the air as she scrambled up from the frozen snow, skittering toward the dog lying at the road's edge.

The sedan spun sideways, jumped the curb and finally came to a stop. The door flew open and a frightened young man sped to their side and knelt beside the dog. "I'm so sorry. I couldn't stop."

"I know," Connor said, trying to calm the distraught man.

Pepper gave a whimper, his tail gave a feeble wag, and he looked at Connor with confused eyes.

Connor tried to examine the terrier without moving him, but before he could make a prognosis, Aunt Phyllis's bellow filled the air. "He's alive," Connor called over his shoulders.

Caitlin knelt beside the terrier, her eyes filled with tears, and Connor didn't know which way to turn. His aunt's cries came from behind, Caitlin's whimper at his left side, and the groans of the young man on his right.

Ellene came to his aid and rushed toward Aunt Phyllis to help her over the slippery lawn.

"My poor Pepper, she moaned, her voice drawing nearer. "My poor puppy."

When she reached Connor's side, Pepper's tail gave a fleeting beat against the ground before he shook his head and rose on wobbly legs.

"Now that's a spunky dog," Connor said, relieved to see the terrier stand.

"Is he okay?" the young man asked. He dug into his pocket and pulled out his driver's license. "I live right up the street. Is there anything I can do?"

Connor glanced at the license, then at his

aunt's face, still filled with panic.

"Is he all right, Connor?" she asked.

"He's stunned, but I think he's fine. We'll see if we can find a vet to check him over."

His aunt looked so weak he grasped her arm. "I'll let you know," he told the driver.

"Here's my business card," the man said, pulling it from his wallet. "I'll be happy to pay the vet's bill. I love animals. I wouldn't hurt a —"

Connor touched his arm with his free hand. "That's okay. We saw you try to stop." He took the man's card and glanced at it. "This is fine. We'll let you know how the dog is."

The neighbor scribbled his home telephone number on his business card, then stood watching as Ellene helped Aunt Phyllis toward the house and he carried the dog with Caitlin clinging to his jacket.

Once inside, he set Pepper on the floor. The dog gave a little whimper and hobbled toward his water dish. Connor studied him, feeling assured the dog wasn't badly injured.

Aunt Phyllis stood over Pepper, her head shaking as badly as her hands. "You'll take him to the vet?"

"Do we have one on the island?" Connor asked.

She paused, her gaze searching above his

head. "No, but we have a retired doctor. I'll call him and see if he'll take a look at Pepper. He's a member of our church."

Connor sidled a look at Ellene. She turned away as if fearing she might chuckle at the picture of a medical doctor examining a dog. To his surprise, in a few minutes his aunt had contacted the man, and he'd agreed.

"I'll go with Connor," Ellene said, crouching beside Pepper. "I'll hold him on my lap."

"I want to go," Caitlin said, hovering over the dog.

"You can stay with Aunt Phyllis, Cait. We won't be long, I promise."

"Okay, Aunt Phyllis and I will play Old Maid while you're gone. That way we won't be worried."

"Sounds good to me, honey," Connor said, bending down to kiss his daughter's cheek. He slipped on his jacket, lifted the terrier into his arms and looked at Ellene. "Ready?"

She nodded.

"What's the doctor's name?" Connor asked.

Aunt Phyllis looked up from the slip of paper where she'd been writing the address. "Dr. Shepherd. Dr. Ralph Shepherd."

"Shepherd? That's appropriate," Connor

said, gazing at the poor dog.

Pepper gave a whimper, and Connor hurried from the house, fearing his aunt would begin another fuss. Ellene closed the door behind him, and he could hear her chuckle as they headed for his SUV.

CHAPTER ELEVEN

"How is he?" Aunt Phyllis said, jumping up from the table and spilling the Old Maid cards to the floor.

"You ruined our game," Caitlin said, then rallied when she spotted the terrier. "Pepper!" She leaped from the chair and bounded toward the dog.

Ellene stood back, observing the homecoming. Her fear had subsided at the doctor's home when Pepper had perked up, seeing the physician. Ellene felt a weight lift from her. An injured animal broke her heart.

"He's fine. Just a few bruises." He tousled the dog's head and put his cheek against his fur.

Ellene had watched Connor's frustration with the terrier since she'd arrived, but tonight Connor's gentle heart touched her.

"He'll be stiff for a few days," Connor said, lowering the dog to the floor and giving his back a pat.

"What do I owe you?" Aunt Phyllis said, crouching beside Pepper and running her work-worn hands over the terrier's fur.

"No charge. Dr. Shepherd said it was a payback for your casserole at the last potluck supper."

His aunt tittered. "He did love it. I think he ate three helpings."

Ellene wondered if Aunt Phyllis was doing a little matchmaking for herself with her casserole. Ellene had always heard the adage the way to a man's heart was through his stomach. "Is Dr. Shepherd a single gentleman?"

"A widower." Aunt Phyllis looked at her, then turned her attention to the dog.

If Ellene was seeing clearly, Connor's aunt had flushed. She gave an inward chuckle as she set her purse on the kitchen counter, then slipped off her jacket and hung it on a hook near the door.

She returned to the circle of sympathy and rested her hand on Aunt Phyllis's shoulder. "He's going to be fine, Aunt Phyllis."

The older woman boosted herself up by pushing her hands against her knees and rose. " 'Look at the birds of the air; they do not sow or reap or store away in barns, and yet your heavenly Father feeds them.' I'm ashamed I worried," she said, folding her arms and gazing at Pepper. "God cares for all creatures. I don't think I even prayed for my puppy."

"But Jesus knew you were sad, and He made Pepper better," Caitlin said, crouching beside the terrier.

"Let's pray now," Aunt Phyllis said, lowering her head. Ellene glanced at Connor's expression and contained a grin as she lowered her head.

"Heavenly Father," Aunt Phyllis said, "thank You for Pepper's safety. We praise You for all good things. For life and love and family. In Jesus' precious name."

They joined in the amen, and Ellene studied Connor's aunt, wondering if it had been her imagination or had she stressed the words *love* and *family.*

Caitlin slipped to the sofa and plopped onto the cushion "I love playing Old Maid, but not as much as I love Pepper."

Pepper heard his name and hobbled over to the sofa to sniff at Caitlin's feet.

"Can he have a treat?"

"Better not, Cait. The doctor gave him a pain shot and it might make him sick," Connor said as he sank into a chair.

Caitlin gazed at the dog for a moment before she settled back, Pepper curling up beside her.

Ellene followed him and sat beside Caitlin.

"The ferry will be open tomorrow," Aunt Phyllis said from the dining-room table. "They'll have it cleared by morning."

Morning. Ellene's belly tightened. Tomorrow she had no more reason to stay. She'd be going home.

The conversation drifted above her thoughts, and when she roused herself, Connor had moved to the fireplace to build a fire.

Caitlin had curled up on the sofa, her eyes heavy from the traumatic events of the day, and Ellene brushed her palm along Caitlin's legs, soothing her.

Morning was closing in with each tick of the clock, and Ellene wavered between relief and sadness. She studied the child's dark-blond hair twining on her face, her spindly arms that gave great hugs nestled against her chest. Her gray eyes hid behind closed lids, but Ellene knew them well. They were as beguiling as Connor's.

"Caitlin," Connor said, leaning over the child. "Time for bed."

She groaned a little and pulled herself tighter into a ball.

"Cait." He brushed the hair from her face. "Do you want me to carry you upstairs?"

Her eyelids tightened, and Connor gave Ellene a fleeting grin before he hoisted the child into his arms.

"Can you get her up the stairs?" Ellene asked.

"We'll see," he said, winking.

"I'll be behind you," Aunt Phyllis said. "Good night, Ellene."

"Good night, Aunt Phyllis. The bed's yours tonight. I'll stay on the sofa. I've gotten used to it."

Connor's aunt gave her a knowing look and headed up the stairs.

Ellene rose and added a log to the fire, then nestled into the corner of the sofa, thinking about the past week and all that had happened. She thought of her frustration when her father had forced her to work with Connor. She recalled her galloping pulse when she realized that her heart had headed in a direction she didn't want it to go. She imagined tomorrow when she'd say goodbye.

Connor's footsteps triggered her attention. His shadow spread across the floor as he headed for the fireplace.

"I just put on a log," she said.

He halted and gazed at the flames a moment as if making certain the log would catch, then stepped back toward the sofa. "Thanks."

She heard a note of melancholy in his voice. "Is she sleeping?"

"Probably not, but she got a free ride upstairs."

Ellene smiled and, on impulse, reached over to caress his hand. Before she pulled it back, Connor cupped her hand in his.

"Not wanting to sound like my aunt, but sometimes I really believe God makes things happen for a purpose."

She didn't question his meaning. The same thought had bounded through her mind so many times since she'd come, but while her heart wanted to accept Connor's friendship, her logic headed in the opposite direction. Friendship was one thing, but she knew the relationship would move on to something more serious.

"You're quiet," Connor said, caressing her fingers with his thumb. He scooted closer and slid his free arm along the back of the sofa.

Ellene had a driving urge to rest her head on his shoulder. Years ago they'd sat late at night in front of her parents' fireplace, nestled in each other's arms.

Connor drew her closer. "I can't thank you enough for pushing Caitlin out of the way, and I surprised myself when I felt bad for that irritating dog."

"I know." She grinned. "You can bark all you want, but you have a tender heart, Mr. Faraday."

"I don't hide it well, do I?"

Her thoughts grew serious. "If anything had happened to Caitlin, I would never have forgiven myself. I'd gone out to keep her company, and I felt responsible."

"I let her go. It wouldn't have been your fault."

"But I'd feel responsible."

"I've felt just like that, Ellene, trying to be a father when I didn't know how to be one. The responsibility, the fear, the love. It all rolls into one tight ball in my stomach. I feel like a man walking a tightrope without knowing how. It's been difficult."

"You've done a beautiful job. She's a lovely child."

"Not before you came into our lives. You got a taste of Caitlin's behavior when you first arrived. I feel at a loss when she's so unhappy, and I don't know what to do."

"You do the best you can." She shifted on her hip to face him. "She needs special attention, and I know that's difficult to give when you're trying to earn a living. Don't punish yourself for your inexperience. All parents begin that way. No one knows what they're doing."

She shifted her hand and wove her fingers through his. "Do you realize you can get lessons in ballet dancing, fencing, public speaking, weaving baskets, using a computer, but you can't really get lessons on being a parent? At least, not lessons that answer all the questions, and then when things go wrong, you have no tech support."

He chuckled and squeezed her hand. "You're right about that."

Connor rested his head against the cushion and she followed as her heart led her, resting her head beside his, their foreheads touching.

He was silent too long. "What's wrong, Connor?"

"I'm just thinking again that I make a rotten father. I —"

Ellene raised her head and looked at him. "Connor, why do you keep saying that? A while ago you started to say something similar, and it bothered me. I'd forgotten until now. You were talking about Caitlin and you asked how you were supposed to raise a child alone, and then it sounded as if you were going to say you hadn't wanted Caitlin. I don't understand why you'd even think such a thing."

Connor lowered his head in his hands. "I didn't mean it that way." He lifted his downcast face and gazed at her. "I'm sorry you heard that."

Ellene's heart skipped, fearing his response. "Why would you say that, Connor?"

He drew in a lengthy breath, and she steeled herself.

He shook his head, his face pale in the flickering light. "I — I . . . I can't explain it, Ellene."

"Why not?"

Sorrow filled his eyes, and her heart felt as if it would break.

"I shouldn't have been a father. I wasn't a good husband."

"But why?"

She felt him tense.

"Because — because I didn't love Melissa the way I should have."

"But you married her."

"Yes." He turned his head away. "I married her —" He sat in silence a moment. "I married her on the rebound. When Melissa died, I figured having to raise Caitlin alone was my punishment for getting married."

His look broke her heart. Tears rolled down her cheeks from her personal guilt and for her sorrow for him. "Connor, I didn't know what I did to you."

He captured her chin in his hand, and his eyes spoke an unknown emotion — something deep and confusing to Ellene.

"I did it to myself," he said.

She wanted to understand, and she sensed he had more to tell, but when she looked at him, his lips moved closer to hers, and her heart rose to her throat, wanting the kiss, yet fearing it. When his mouth touched hers, she melted into his embrace as if she'd finally come home.

Connor drew her closer, their pulses beating in unison. When he eased back, his gaze still bound to hers, she felt tears brim her lashes. For so many years, she fought the dream of being in Connor's arms again. She'd carried the weight of anger and pain that she alone had caused with her self-centeredness.

Connor brushed tears from her cheeks. The look in his eyes played games with her heart. She nestled beside him and gazed at the fireplace.

The fire had become embers. A red glow sparked from the floor of the hearth with an occasional burst of flame, like the eruptions of guilt that burned in her conscience. "Connor, I fell in love a couple years ago," she blurted.

He stiffened and looked at her as if con-founded.

"It ended. I was hurt."

"What happened?" he asked, looking at her as if he assumed she'd been the one to end the relationship.

"He walked out on me."

"He did?"

She knew she'd been right about his earlier thought, and she couldn't blame him. The idea had never registered that Owen had treated her no worse than she'd treated Connor . . . except for the intimacy. The memory ached within her.

"I'm sorry." His voice had softened, and he eased closer to her side. "I'm really sorry. It hurts either way."

Either way. His meaning was clear, but she accepted it. Connor was right. She only nodded, unable to respond.

He leaned closer and kissed her, a brief caress that assured her he understood.

He stretched and glanced at his watch. "Time for bed. What do you think?"

She nodded, sensing going to bed was his way of controlling his emotions, but she agreed. She had so much to think about.

Connor rose, still holding her hand. "I'll see you in the morning."

"Morning," she repeated, feeling his

fingers loose from hers, leaving her feeling empty and alone.

His shadow vanished through the doorway, and she heard him in the bathroom, running water. Soon his bedroom door closed.

Ellene made up the sofa, then lay there accompanied by guilt and dreams. How could she make things right with him? She had to tell him the whole story, but she feared the ramifications.

Her lips felt swollen from their kisses and the pressure lingered on her mouth. She touched her lips, remembering the joy that filled her, sensing that maybe God truly had had a part in their reunion.

She tossed and turned, longing for sleep, enjoying the feeling of being cherished, yet afraid because it meant trusting and being totally honest.

The fireplace glow faded to a sprinkle of ash, and she pulled the blanket up around her ears, listening to the night sounds while wishing that Connor were at her side to tell her what to do, but he was the reason for her dilemma. Only God could give her courage and directions.

For now, she waded through her fears. Could a commitment work? Could she trust

Connor? Panic stifled her.

Connor tossed in bed, watching shadows crawl on the ceiling, his mind riled by his confession. How would Ellene have taken the whole story? She'd looked misty-eyed, but when she gave it more thought would she think him crude for what he did? And if he told her everything would she turn on him again? He'd been a coward not to tell her about Caitlin tonight while she seemed open to hearing.

He admitted his faith had been weak, truly more like non-existent, but he believed now, and the sin sat hard on his conscience.

Tears brimmed his eyes. He should have been candid tonight and get it out in the open. When Melissa had told him she was pregnant, he'd felt tricked and used. She wanted a husband, and he'd fallen for the bait. He'd resented Melissa's pregnancy. He'd thought of walking away and leaving her with the problem. He knew he hadn't been the only man in her life.

He'd felt like a misfit when he'd first lain with her, trying to act as though he knew what to do. She'd caught on and taught him how to be a man, a humbling experience and even more so, a heartbreaking one.

He'd longed to share that intimacy first with Ellene.

Ellene's confession had startled him, but he knew it shouldn't have. She was a beautiful woman, and he could only guess how many men found her desirable. He wondered if her chastity had ended their relationship. In today's world, he'd learned that few women held their virginity sacred.

Ellene surprised him at every turn, especially her deep feelings for Caitlin. He'd watched them together, a kind of intimacy he didn't understand. He was the breadwinner, the father who protected and supported his child, but he didn't know how to be a confidant and a playmate. His mind worked differently than Caitlin's. Her needs were different.

Caitlin's need broke his heart. His little daughter wanted to be like so many others, with a mother and father. How could a man provide all the needs of a daughter?

But with Ellene, they'd melded together like peanut butter and jelly, a perfect combination. He'd watched them giggling together. Caitlin mimicked Ellene's every move, and what would she do tomorrow when Ellene drove away?

Last night, Ellene had kissed him with the fervor he remembered from their youth, but tomorrow would those kisses remain a memory? When the daylight brightened the sky, would the outcome darken his world again?

He wondered if Ellene were awake, thinking of what he'd told her about not being a good husband. She'd changed too since she'd arrived. Her business persona had finally thawed into something warmer and more caring until she remembered. Then the business tone returned, but the past few days, since their truce, she'd become the real woman he'd loved, yet with greater wisdom and a new depth.

He squeezed his eyes shut, concentrating on sleep. His thoughts drifted to the Lord and what He wanted from Connor's life. Could it be, Lord? Do You have some purpose in mind for me? For Ellene? Take compassion on Caitlin, Father. Don't let her heart be broken with Ellene's leaving. A chill skittered up his back, and he tucked the blanket around himself. "And my heart, too, Lord. Don't let it be broken, either."

Somewhere in the night Connor knew he had drifted to sleep because a noise from the great room roused him. He sat up and looked at the clock. It was after seven. He bolted from bed, slipped on his pants and shirt, then opened his door.

Ellene stood near the table, dressed and holding a coffee mug. "Good morning," she said, when he came through the archway.

"Are you going already?"

"I thought so."

"How about breakfast?"

"Coffee's fine." She set the cup on the table. "I didn't want to leave without saying goodbye and thanking you for your hospitality."

Hospitality? She made it sound as if she were an ordinary guest who'd stopped by for the evening. "It's been our pleasure. You know that."

"It's had its moments." A faint smile curved her lips.

Her lips. His memory soared back to the past evening in front of the fire. How could he shake hands and say goodbye?

"The ferry's running. I called awhile ago. I'll be in touch as soon as I get an architect to draw up the plans, and I'll send you an estimate in a couple of days."

Bewildered, his arms plopped to his sides. "What about last night?"

She fiddled in her handbag for something and didn't look up.

"Ellene, what about last night?"

She inched her head upward. "I need to

think, Connor. This place is bewitching. I'm confused. It's like a vacation when everything seems perfect. It's not real when you put it into everyday life."

"It shouldn't confuse you. Don't try to make sense out of it. Emotions aren't always logical. They're in here." He patted his hand against his chest.

"I know," she said, shaking her head and pressing her palm against her chest. "I feel it in there, but it could be as fleeting as a comet — awesome, but the fire is out in a moment."

He saw no point in trying to convince her. Ellene could be stubborn as a cat. She would have her own way. "You're not going to leave without saying goodbye to Caitlin."

She picked up an envelope from the table. "I wrote her a note."

"A note?" He stared at her, disbelieving. "She's six. A note isn't what she needs."

"I'm not sure I have what she needs. I'll see her again. I made a promise, and I'll keep it."

She lifted the laptop from the chair seat and headed for the door, then turned back. "Connor, last night I lay awake most of the night amazed at what had happened. I need to make sense out of it all."

"Are you stuck in the past again, Ellene?"

"Last night I asked myself what would happen if things blossomed, and we decided to try again. We can't just be friends, Connor. No way. We have too much past, but I'm not sure we have a future. We need to think about this carefully. I don't want to hurt anyone else again, and I definitely don't want to suffer again if we make a mistake."

"Did you ever think walking away now could be the mistake? Did you consider that?"

She lowered her head a moment. "Yes. I've made too many bad decisions in my short lifetime, and I don't want to make another. Trust me on this."

"How can I? I trusted you once, and you threw the trust back in my face."

She put her hand on the doorknob. "I'm sorry." She pulled opened the door and turned back. "Say goodbye to your aunt, too. Tell her I learned a lot from her."

"I'm not sure you did," he said.

She gave him a piercing look, pushed open the storm door and stepped outside.

The cold morning whisked past him, less icy than the look in Ellene's eyes.

CHAPTER TWELVE

Connor caved onto the sofa and stared at the envelope. It stung that Ellene had written Caitlin a note to say goodbye.

He stared into space, trying to make sense out of it all. What had happened? Why had she changed so radically from the night before?

He didn't know how long he'd sat there. The next sounds he heard were his aunt and Caitlin's footsteps on the stairs. He swallowed the emotion that rose in his throat, picturing his daughter's reaction.

"Daddy," she said, skipping away from the stairs, her arms open to greet him.

He drew her in, holding her close and wanting to protect her.

"Where's Ellene?" his aunt asked.

He shifted his gaze from Caitlin to his aunt, then back to Caitlin. "She left early."

"She left," Caitlin said, her smile fading to distress. "But she didn't say goodbye."

His aunt wandered to the kitchen counter for a mug of coffee. "She made coffee."

"Ellene left you a note," he said, handing the envelope to Caitlin.

Caitlin stared at it for a moment with a look that tore at his heart. Finally she took it from him and turned it over in her hands as if not knowing what to do with it.

"Open the flap," he said.

She tucked her finger beneath it and pulled up. The paper tore, and she struggled to release the note. She gazed at it a moment, then handed it to him. "I can't read it."

"It's in cursive," he said, knowing that even if Ellene had printed it, Caitlin could probably only sound out some of the words.

"Read it to me, Daddy."

Tears brimmed her lashes, and her sad eyes squeezed his heart, and he lowered his gaze to the paper.

Dear Caitlin,
I'm sorry I have to leave so early. I must get home so I can go to work.

"Today's Sunday. She doesn't work on Sunday."

"I know," he said, "but she probably has things to do to get ready for work."

She lowered her eyes and seemed to ponder what he said, then raised her head. "What else does it say?"

He looked at the letter again.

I promised I would see you again, and I will. In a week or so, I will be back to show you all the plans for the cottage.

"But I don't want plans," Caitlin whimpered. "I want to play Old Maid and go outside for walks when the snow melts. I want to go to the store and buy more tops so we can be twins."

"Shush," Connor said, trying to control the emotion charging through him. He wanted to remind her once again that people didn't always get what they wanted, but he'd fallen into the same trap. He wanted Ellene, too, and he'd really thought that maybe this time . . .

"Read the rest, Daddy."

I had so much fun meeting you and playing Old Maid, and you were so brave when you tried to save Pepper from the car. I was very proud of you. Until I see you again, be a good girl and here are

some hugs for you.
O O O O O O

Love,
Ellene.

Connor knelt down to show Caitlin the circles. "Those are hugs."

"They are?" Caitlin asked.

"And Xs are kisses." He forced himself to smile. "I'll put Xs on your cheeks." He leaned toward her and kissed each moist cheek.

Caitlin brushed the teary kisses from her face, and ducked away, then grabbed her letter from his hand. "She should have given me the hugs for real."

Aunt Phyllis mumbled her agreement under her breath, but Connor overheard her.

Caitlin sat at the table, the letter beside her cereal bowl. She drank some milk and ate only a few spoons of cereal. Her eyes looked distant, and she didn't speak.

Connor couldn't eat, and the longer he thought about it, the more disappointed he became. Ellene had given him the brush-off once before, and this time she'd left not only him but Caitlin. He would never let her hurt him or Caitlin again.

■ ■ ■ ■

Ellene sat in her car, feeling the bumpy ferry ride across the channel. Her car jolted, letting her know they'd reached land. She turned her head and looked through the rear window, seeing the island sitting with sprawling fingers on Lake St. Clair.

She ached. Her sleepless night weighed against her spirit; she wished she had slept and awakened feeling uplifted, but she hadn't. She'd awakened more confused than ever.

She'd succumbed to Connor. She'd heard his story, and though she understood, she felt cheated that she hadn't been the one to experience the sacred giving of her body and her heart. That was to have happened on their wedding night.

Connor still believed she'd remained chaste. His assuredness touched her and then angered her. Had he presumed she had no emotion? Had he thought it had been easy for her to walk away from his kisses, longing for more, yet knowing being chaste was what God expected?

His faith had begun to grow. How could she tell him now that she'd failed as a Christian? She feared disillusioning him and turning him against her and the Lord. She couldn't allow that to happen.

She'd bungled things again. Tears filled her eyes, and as she watched the cars move in front of her, she started her car and rolled down the ramp with her eyes blurring.

She turned on the radio and adjusted the dial until she heard a hymn she loved. Sunday. Last Sunday she'd listened to Aunt Phyllis's sermon about forgiveness and family. Today she'd forgotten every word and let her deep-seated fears uproot the lesson the scripture had planted.

She thought of Christine Powers. She punched in her number, figuring she'd be home on a Sunday morning. When Ellene heard her friend's voice, she felt tears rim her eyes. "I blew it."

"Ellene?"

"I really messed things up badly."

"What did you do?"

"It's too complicated to talk over the phone. Are you home for a while?"

"Yes. No plans. Where are you?"

Ellene's hands tightened on the steering wheel. "I just left the Harsens Island ferry."

"Just now? You're kidding. What happened?"

"I'll tell you when I get there."

"Drive carefully."

What happened? Christine's words hung in her mind. She didn't know what had happened.

An hour later, she pulled up in front of Christine's condo and wondered why she'd come. Her friend couldn't do a thing to change what she'd done, and Ellene wasn't sure she wanted to. She lowered her head against the steering wheel, trying to sort through the positives and negatives, the goods and bads she'd experienced with Connor.

She ignored the past events, and instead thought about her week on the island. She envisioned Connor and his love for Caitlin, his frustration in not knowing how to be a good father and mother. He was open about his behavior after they'd broken up, and he'd defended her chastity.

Accepting Connor into her life meant either honesty and beginning on a clean slate or spending her life in a lie. The lie seemed easier, but the truth seemed the only way.

A rap on the window gave her a start. She lifted her head from the wheel and saw Christine's concerned face.

"Are you okay?" her friend asked.

She nodded, unlocked the door and stepped to the ground.

Christine's fist was knotted against her chest. "You gave me a fright. I thought you'd died or something the way your head was resting on the wheel."

"Sorry," she said, giving her friend a hug. "I was trying to make sense out of my life."

Christine linked arms with her and led her up the condo's sidewalk. "Come inside so we can talk."

In the living room, Ellene settled in an easy chair that faced the picture window.

"So tell me what happened," Christine said, curling her legs under her on the sofa.

Ellene's mind flew in a variety of directions, lingering on things she'd thought about in the car and other moments that came to mind that could have made her smile if not for the pain she felt.

She related her experiences on the island, all those goods and bads that she'd thought about earlier, except she struggled to find the bads because they were all in the past.

"What is it about him that bothers you now?" Christine asked, leaning forward as if trying to understand.

"Nothing really. We had a disagreement about his business plans, but that was like any argument. We just had different ideas."

"Is it the child?"

"Caitlin? No. Not at all." Hearing Caitlin's name in her thoughts sent Ellene's stomach on a wild elevator ride. "I'm crazy about her. She's so loving, and she emulates nearly everything I do. Her earlier behavior shocked me, but after I was there a couple of days, she was a changed child."

Christine leaned back against the cushion. "You were a good influence."

"I was, but now —" Connor's words rose in her mind. *Caitlin will feel abandoned when you leave.* "I'm afraid of how she'll react when she finds out I'm gone."

Christine frowned. "You mean you didn't say goodbye?"

"She was sleeping. I didn't want to wake her."

"That was almost cruel, Ellene, if you meant that much to her."

"I left her a note."

Christine rose and shook her head. She strode across the room and spun around to face her. "You left a note for a six-year-old? What were you thinking? Even an adult can't handle a Dear John letter very well."

Christine's frustration weighed on her. She knew her friend was right. She'd let Caitlin down in the worst way. "But I promised I'd see her again."

"Promises can be broken. How can she trust you when she couldn't trust you to say goodbye? She's lost a mother. She's leery about people vanishing from her life. Now you've vanished — at least in her eyes. How do you think that will set with a six-year-old?"

Tears formed in Ellene's eyes and rolled down her cheeks. "I don't know. I can't get beyond myself. I'm only focusing on what hurts me and not on what hurts others."

Christine hurried forward and sat on the arm of the chair, putting her arm around Ellene's shoulders. "You've made a big step just realizing that. We all do it. Some of us face our needs first, then if it's not inconvenient we see what others need. I've done the same. I'm no one to judge you, but that's what happened."

Ellene brushed the tears from her cheeks. "I'll keep my promise with Caitlin. She'll know she can trust me, but I can't stop her from sticking to me like glue, and if I can't settle things with Connor, she'll still be hurt."

"You can take that chance, and if that's the case, you can let her know that you still love her. You can do something to make it better. I'm no child psychologist, but I know you can find a way to make things better."

"And Connor . . . I'm telling you, Christine, the man's in my blood, but I'm so afraid. I lay in bed all night before I left, reliving his confession, his hon esty. I could still feel his arms around me, his lips on mine. I can still see the look in his eyes."

"The eyes have it," Christine said. She was trying to be lighthearted, but it didn't work.

"The Bible says something about the lamp of the body is the eyes. It's as if looking into Connor's eyes, I can see his soul."

"Do you like what you see?"

"I do."

"Then what's the problem?"

"Me. I'm the problem."

Christine gave her a hug. "You can fix that."

Connor sat beside Rudolph Long and signed the purchase agreement. Checks exchanged hands, and he left the office, owner of Island Sports Shop.

Over a week had passed since he'd seen Ellene, but she'd called him twice to check on details for the architect who was designing the plans. She'd asked about Caitlin, and he'd out-and-out lied. He'd told her she was great, which was far from the truth, but other than asking about his daughter, she'd been strictly business.

He'd made a decision the day Ellene left. Connor had hit his third strike. It was in

Ellene's ballpark now.

He laid the paperwork on the passenger seat, turned the key in the ignition and pulled away from the real-estate office.

Since Ellene's biting remarks about the sport store, he'd wavered in his thinking. The business had been his dream. He'd felt confident, but she'd knocked the edge off his fine-honed plans. Determined not to fail, he'd made a new plan, and this one had given him a bigger boost than he could have imagined.

He pulled his cell phone from the SUV's cup holder and punched in the number. After he'd made it past the secretary, he waited, a smile growing on his face.

"Hi. Mr. Bordini, this is Connor."

"How'd it go?"

"It's a done deal," he said, trying not to laugh into the receiver, but his spirit had lifted more than he could have imagined.

"Good for you, son. Hang on a minute."

Connor heard the shuffling sound of a muffled phone and heard a woman's voice, then silence.

"I'm back," Syl Bordini said. "That was Ellene just now. She has your plans about ready, and she's going to call you to set an appointment."

"Good. I'm anxious to get started." He

tried to keep a controlled tone in his voice, but even a mention of Ellene sent him reeling. He forced the question from his throat. "Does she know about —"

"This is business between you and me, son."

Connor tried to read what he was really saying.

"When do you have to be out of the house?" Syl Bordini asked.

"The first week in June. That means Caitlin can finish school in St. Clair Shores without any problems."

"Good news."

Connor returned to the purpose for his call. "I thought I'd stop in when I get to town. I have some paperwork on the new products and some ideas that I wanted to go over with you. Let you take a look and give me your opinion."

Syl cleared his throat. "Connor, it's not that I don't care, but we have an agreement that you run the shop and make the decisions. I'm only a —"

"I know, sir, but I respect your comments and your expertise. I wouldn't have talked to you if I didn't."

"I'm always happy to be a sounding board. Listen —"

Connor heard Syl's voice shift from the

phone, then a rustle of paper.

"Okay. Here's an idea. I'm having some company in on Saturday. Stop by for dinner around six. Bring Caitlin if you'd like. You might as well get a meal out of it."

Connor's stomach twisted. He hadn't wanted to make a social event out of it. He'd planned to keep things purely business, just as Ellene was doing, but how could he refuse his business partner? "That sounds fine. I'll see you then."

When he hung up, he forced himself to focus on the new shop, and all his ideas. Ellene had given him good advice. He took the time to analyze what had gone wrong with the shop as it stood, and the problems were obvious. He wondered if Ellene would admire him more when she learned he'd studied the store before jumping into an agreement. If he didn't have her love, he coveted her respect.

As the thought sat in his mind, he struck his palm against the steering wheel. Why did he care about Ellene's opinion on anything? She'd undermined his life so far. Why would he think she would try to ruin his business?

He shook his head. *Lord, give me patience and forgiveness. I don't want to be vindictive and I've already taken a step in that direction*

205

by soliciting her father's aid. Help me be the model of a Christian man and learn to turn the other cheek.

"Happy birthday, Ellene." Her aunt Teresa grabbed Ellene's cheeks and kissed her.

"Thanks," Ellene said, accepting her aunt's package and setting it on the foyer table. "Let me take your jacket."

Her aunt waved her away. "You go ahead. Uncle Gino is parking the car. I'll let him take it upstairs."

Ellene grasped the gift and carried it into the living room, setting it in front of the fireplace where other gifts had been piled.

She hated birthday parties. She felt as if she were ten, especially now when she hadn't been in the mood for anything like this. But her mother had insisted — a nice little family dinner. The word *little* wasn't in the vocabulary of an Italian family. Already her aunt Carmela and uncle Donato had arrived along with their son Tito and his wife.

Cold hands covered her eyes, and she could tell who it was from the scent of garlic on his hands. "Uncle Gino. Did you bring flat bread?"

"How'd you guess?" he asked, tweaking her cheek.

"I'm getting smarter with every year." And my nose is getting more sensitive, she mentally added.

Someone had turned on the television, cranking up the volume so it could be heard above their voices. Ellene knew the pattern. The family just talked louder.

"The Tigers are losers," Tito called from the dining room.

Uncle Gino jumped up from his chair and shook his fist. "Don't get smart-mouthed with me," he said, a chuckle in his voice. "I'll give you five bucks if the White Sox win."

"Great. I can use the money," Tito yelled, darting from the room as laughter drowned out the announcer.

The doorbell rang again, and Ellene watched her father answer it. "If it isn't my goombah."

From the greeting, she knew it was a long-time family friend. Seeing an opportunity to slip away, she wove through the family gathered between the living room and kitchen, then stepped onto the enclosed porch. The din seemed muted there.

She leaned against the windowsill, looking out. Spring had finally made an appearance.

Though the temperature was in the low sixties, she saw the promise of trees in bloom and tulips peeking up from the ground. A few more warm days, and spring would surely arrive.

Easter was tomorrow, and the festival always made her think of things being reborn, fresh and new. She'd promised her parents she would go to their worship service tomorrow even though she'd found another congregation she enjoyed more, but the church was too contemporary for her parents.

The noise grew, and Ellene sank into a wicker chair, wondering how Connor was spending his day. She'd spoken to him twice and had been deeply disappointed. His tone was cool and restrained, and she figured he was still angry. Once again she'd thought Connor would have called her. When would she learn?

Her promise to Caitlin filled her mind. She should call Connor and see if he'd let her take Caitlin somewhere. Maybe the zoo once the temperature warmed or — She went blank. Where did people take children?

Ellene rested her elbows on her knees and lowered her face to her hands. She'd messed up again. She was thirty years old today. She would have thought with time she'd learned something.

She hadn't.

Connor pulled up in front of the Bordinis' home and turned off the engine. The house looked the same, except the shutters appeared to be a different color, but he didn't trust his memory. He'd always found their home attractive — a big colonial in Sterling Heights. Randazoo's Produce, Buscemi's Pizza, Papa Vito's Restaurant, Bordini's Construction — Italian businesses abounded in the community.

He hadn't taken up Syl Bordini's offer to bring Caitlin. A dinner party didn't seem an appropriate place for a child. It wasn't even that appropriate for him to be here, since he'd come with business in mind.

He stepped out of the car with a hopeful feeling that spring might be close by. When he gazed down the street at a couple of brave trees beginning to bud, his heart stopped. He squinted, trying to decide if that was Ellene's sedan. He wasn't certain, but it looked like hers.

Connor reached back inside the vehicle and picked up the box of chocolates and the envelope that held the business information for Mr. Bordini.

He headed up the walk, worried that Ellene would make a scene if she saw him there or that she would assume he'd plotted a way to get invited. After pushing the doorbell, he stood waiting, hearing the sounds from inside. Ellene's family. He remembered them all so well. They'd always filled him with food, love and pure joy. Why had he ever doubted that he'd be accepted by the Bordinis?

The door swung open, and Ellene's father greeted him with an enthusiastic handshake. "Come in. Come in," he said, glancing into the living room where the baseball game and the conversation had reached a hundred decibels, he guessed.

"These are for Mrs. Bordini," he said, thrusting the chocolate box toward him.

"Hold on to it. You can give it to her yourself. But first —" Mr. Bordini beckoned him down the hallway. "We can talk in here," he said, closing the door of his home office. "You know family."

"I know yours, sir."

"Connor. We're business partners now. You don't have to call me sir. Plain old Syl will do just fine."

"Thank you, Syl."

"Give me your jacket and tell me what's in that envelope."

Connor set the chocolates on a chair and

slipped off his jacket, then waited until Syl had pulled up a chair near his before he opened the envelope. "First, I studied the shop and the records, then realized what was lacking: winter sports equipment. Summer gear packed the shelves and displays, but I didn't see any orders for cross-country skis, ice skates, sleds, snowmobiles, that kind of thing."

"Any business has to be seasonal," Syl said. "Good observation."

"I realize snowmobiles are an expensive inventory, but I've talked to the owner of a business in Algonac and we might work out a deal. I keep one in stock, and he'll send the snowmobiles in from the mainland. Profit will be lower, but it saves me storage, and it can be a fast turnaround. I could have the snowmobile by the next day."

He nodded his head. "Very practical. Excellent idea."

"Thanks, and I also noticed the shop doesn't carry bicycles. That's a great form of transportation. Exercise equipment is another thought, but these are just my observations."

"You've given it a lot of thought, Connor."

Connor handed Syl the contents from the envelope. "Here's the information. You can look it over. I value your comments."

"You got it," Syl said, rising and placing the documents on his desk. "Now, how about a drink or some appetizers? Mona made some of her specialties. You remember her cheese and prosciutto roll-ups? Dinner will be ready soon." He gave Connor a solid pat on the back.

"That sounds good," Connor said, rising and following him back down the hallway into the living room, carrying the chocolates.

Voices faded as he stepped into a room full of people. The television's volume resounded with a three-base hit for the Tigers while a roar rang through the stadium.

"You remember Connor Faraday," Syl said, shaking his shoulder. "He was Ellene's fiancé."

The title nailed him to the floor. Eyebrows raised, and vaguely familiar faces looked from one to another until a woman stepped forward and clutched his cheeks between her palms.

"Connor. How could we forget?" She kissed him on the mouth. "I'm Ellene's aunt Teresa."

"Yes," he said, more startled than he let on. "It's nice to see you."

Syl grasped his arm and pointed. "Connor, you remember Uncle Gino, Tito and his wife Lucy, Uncle Donato." His arm swung toward the doorway. "Aunt Carmela is in the kitchen." He motioned again. "And my goombah Frankie and his wife Florence."

Connor nodded. "It's nice to see you," he said, shaking hands as he surveyed the room. "And nice to meet you," he added to Frankie and Florence.

"Connor!"

He looked up to see Ellene's mother, Mona, charging across the room, her arms open wide.

"Mrs. Bordini," he said, extending his hand, but that did little good. She wrapped her arms around him in a bear hug.

"It's been too long, Connor. How nice of you to come to Ellene's birthday party."

Birthday party. He faltered, looking at the box of chocolates, but no gift for Ellene. He wanted to sink through the floor.

"Syl didn't tell me it was Ellene's birthday party."

"No?" She eyed her husband, then the chocolates.

"These are for you," he said, wishing he'd brought flowers and candy.

"Thank you, Connor, and what difference if you knew or not. You're a gift for coming." She gestured toward the dining-room buffet through the archway. "Have some hors d'oeuvres. Uncle Gino brought some flat bread. I remember you loved that with the roasted peppers. Dinner will be ready soon."

"Look at that batter run," someone yelled, his eyes riveted on the TV.

Eyes turned from him to the baseball game, and Connor slunk from the room toward the buffet, knowing he would soon find Ellene somewhere in the gathering.

The closer he got to the kitchen the stronger the tantalizing aromas grew. He'd loved meals at the Bordinis' home. Rich pastas with giant-sized meatballs, home-made ravioli, Mona's own fettuccine in alfredo sauce, spinach sautéed in garlic and olive oil. He could go on forever about the wonderful delights he'd had at Ellene's.

As he placed a sample of appetizers on the paper plate, Syl approached him with a hangdog look. "Mona's biting my head off for not telling you the dinner was for Ellene's birthday."

"I wondered why myself." Connor balanced the plate, feeling uncomfortable.

He gave a feeble shrug. "I guessed you and Ellene had a tiff. I figured this could help break the ice."

Connor's voice caught in his throat. "I'm not sure I want to break the ice. I'm sorry, but she's —"

"You don't have to tell me. I know my daughter. She'll see the light, Connor. Give her time." He squeezed Connor's arm and made his way back to the bedlam around the TV.

Connor ambled away from the noise. Fearing he'd see Ellene, he bypassed the kitchen and headed for the enclosed porch where he hoped he could find some solitude to think. Ellene's birthday. He felt like a heel having shown up. And without a gift.

Ellene's father had known he wouldn't come if he'd told him. Connor stood in the threshold of the porch, weighing their conversation. He let the thought simmer as he stepped onto the porch and faltered, seeing Ellene sitting alone. His heart flew to his throat.

Her eyes widened, then squinted into a frown. "What are you doing here?"

"I've asked myself that same question," he said, forcing himself to amble toward her. "I needed to have a brief meeting with your father, and he invited me to stop by. I didn't know it was your birthday party until I got here."

She jerked her head away and folded her

arms across her chest. "Dad! Isn't he a gem?"

"Actually he is, Ellene. He's a good man."

She spun back. "I know that, but he meddles in my life, Connor. I don't need that."

But maybe you do, Connor thought.

"Meeting?" Her scowl broadened. "What kind of a meeting?"

She didn't know. His stomach twisted and he set the plate of appetizers on the wicker table. There was no way he could eat now, and he needed to get out of here.

"Some business. It's between your father and me."

"Business?" She shook her head.

"There you are." Syl's voice boomed from the doorway.

"I should have guessed I'd find you here." He stepped forward and wrapped his arm around Connor's shoulders. "So what do you think, Ellene?"

"Think about what?" she asked, her confused expression growing as she looked from her father to him.

"Our partnership," her father said.

Her mouth gaped. "Partnership? You and Connor?"

"He's got a good head on his shoulders." He gave him a hearty pat again. "I'm giving him moral support."

"And some financial help," Connor added, "until I can take over on my own."

Ellene closed her mouth, but the pinched look remained. "That's nice for you both." She rose and swept past them into the house.

Syl gave him a bewildered look.

Connor offered a feeble smile. "Who can understand a woman?"

He turned back toward the doorway, and Connor followed, fearing Syl had messed things up for good.

CHAPTER THIRTEEN

Ellene stormed into the dining room, over-whelmed by Connor's presence, but the emotion again swung between anger and adulation. A partnership. Her dad and Connor. Though it startled her, Ellene couldn't help but laugh at the absurdity. *What are you doing, Lord?*

She'd missed Connor so much the past two weeks, and once again her pride and stubbornness had kept her from giving in. She wanted to ask him about Caitlin, but even saying her name would bring her to tears.

"I've been looking for you," her mother said, hurrying in from the living room. "Can you help get the food on the table? We want everyone to eat while it's warm."

Ellene nodded and stepped into the kitchen, overtaken by the delicious scents of her mother's cooking. Yet the thought of food shriveled when she pictured Connor at the family table, his smug expression aimed at her.

But Connor hadn't had a smug expression, she recalled. He'd looked as startled as she felt. Maybe he had forgotten her birthday and the situation had been her father's doing. He'd always liked Connor, and she wouldn't put it past him to try and patch their relationship.

She carried the huge salad bowl and Italian dressing to the table, then returned for the pasta and garlic bread.

Her mother brought in a platter of chicken that smelled as if it had fallen into a garlic patch. Aunt Teresa passed her with green beans and mashed potatoes.

A feast for her birthday.

"Mangi. Mangi," her mother called into the living room, to announce it was time to eat.

The family rose, leaving the television on, and came into the dining room. Ellene watched them come through the doorway, their voices in contest to see who could top the next as they settled around the table.

Her stomach tightened, watching for Connor to appear, but he didn't and she feared he'd left after her cold response. Her father took the head of the table and glanced over his shoulder.

Connor finally appeared, apologizing that

219

he'd gone to wash his hands. He sat across from her. Everyone was seated expect her mother who stood near her father at the end of the table.

Her dad bowed his head and the family joined in as he blessed the food and her birthday. As soon as the amen was spoken, arms shot forward to lift dishes of food. The talk began, and Ellene felt overwhelmed by Connor's face across the table and her inability to speak with him, to apologize or to at least ask about Caitlin.

"Buon appetito!" her father called, raising his glass. The others repeated his good wishes on the food, and the dishes passed as each filled their plates. Ellene pushed her food around, longing to enjoy the delicious meal. Her mother walked around the table, moving the dishes from one spot to another, refilling empty platters, and hovering over the table.

"Eat something, Mom," Ellene said. She knew her mother wouldn't listen. It was the Italian way for the hostess to wait on the table until others ate. Then her mother would grab a plate and eat in the kitchen as she rinsed the dirty dishes. She'd seen the same at her aunt Teresa's and aunt Carmela's. It was the Italian way, and she was glad she'd been born into a new generation that didn't find it necessary.

She glanced at Connor when she thought he was looking the other direction or concentrating on his meal. His appetite didn't seem much better than hers. He looked up and caught her watching him. He looked away without a blink. The disinterest jarred her.

Ellene wanted to scream. Her feelings were as tangled as the fettuccine on the platter. Each emotion wrapped around another until she couldn't find where one ended and one began. How could she love someone and push him away at the same time?

He made her heart flutter with his look, but her mind burned with frustration. Who caused her frustration? Was it really Connor or was she to blame?

The torment finally ended. People rose with the promise of dessert later. She'd seen the cake her mother had purchased at Sweetheart Bakery. Her favorite — cherry nut. They used that for wedding cakes she'd learned awhile ago. It was hard to think about wedding cakes with Connor here.

She piled the dirty dishes into a stack and carried them to the kitchen, then returned for more. The baseball game continued with plays bellowed out by Tito or one of her uncles. She loved her family, but today she wanted to wring someone's neck. Maybe her own.

With perspiration moistening her hairline from the hot water and the crowd of women in the kitchen, Ellene made her way into the living room. She scanned the faces for Connor's. Then through the window, she saw his car pull away. Her heart dropped, and she closed her eyes, knowing she'd dug herself deeper into an unending pit.

Her father gave her a questioning look. "Connor said to say goodbye. He had to pick up Caitlin."

Ellene nodded and slipped away, heading for a quiet place. She found her father's office empty. She closed the door and sank into the desk chair. An envelope lay on the top with Connor's handwriting.

She shifted her hands to the flap, lifted it, then let it drop. This wasn't her business. If she wanted to know more, she would have to ask her father. It was time she acted like an adult, and not the spoiled child that Connor had accused her of being so long ago.

He'd been right.

Connor didn't know if he was making a mistake or not, but he pulled into the

Harvest Christian Church parking lot and turned off the ignition.

"Why are we coming to this church?" Caitlin asked, staring at the unfamiliar building.

"This is where Ellene's parents go to church."

Caitlin's eyes brighten. "Is Ellene here?"

"Maybe," he said, hoping that what he'd overheard yesterday was true. "Today's Easter, and —"

"I know it's Easter," she said. "Jesus wakes up from the dead on Easter."

"That's right, Cait. You're very smart."

She grinned. "He was in a tomb. Dead."

"Uh-huh," he said, waiting while she unlatched her seatbelt.

"But he wasn't dead anymore. He walked out of the tomb because God let him."

He agreed as he locked the car door.

"How come Mom didn't rise up from the dead?"

The question smacked him between the eyes. Why now? He watched the people scurrying into the church and knew worship was about to begin. He'd hoped to get inside early enough to —

"Why not, Daddy?"

He looked at his daughter's questioning eyes and drew her closer as they walked.

"Your mom did rise from the dead, but she rose all the way to heaven. She's living with Jesus now. Remember? We talked about this before."

"I know, but why didn't she get to come back for a while so I could have seen her before she went to heaven? Jesus did."

"We can't tell God how to do things, Cait. We have to trust Him."

"And trust His promises."

"You're more than smart, sweetheart. You're brilliant."

Caitlin leaned against his hip as they reached the building. Connor took her hand as they climbed the steps into the church. Inside, the scent of Easter lilies permeated the vestibule.

When they entered the sanctuary, he stopped, amazed at the display of lilies and tulips that filled the worship area. A huge lily cross stood before them all. Tulips and lilies lined the recessed windows.

A banner hung from the front wall, declaring, He Is Risen. Hallelujah! Sidewall banners announced other messages: Rejoice!, He Is Risen Indeed and My Redeemer Lives.

Preoccupied with the church's decorations, he slid into a row without looking for Ellene and her family. Once seated, Connor

224

searched and realized they weren't in front of him. Not wanting his curiosity to draw attention to itself, he didn't turn to look behind him. When the first song began, he opened the hymnal.

The joyful Easter hymns were familiar and the choral music echoed through the large beams overhead. The eternal Easter message uplifted him, and the prayers surrounded him with hope. When the service ended, he no longer cared if Ellene was present. The traditional service had given him what he needed. Jesus had died for his sins, and he had plenty to be forgiven. He could rest in that promise.

Caitlin skipped beside him in her new dress. She had grown so much in the past year. Soon his little girl would be fighting off young men, and he prayed she had the same strong Christian values that Ellene had. He could only teach her, then let his teachings guide her actions.

When they stepped outside into the sunshine, Connor's thoughts shifted back to the icy island only weeks earlier. Strange how the weather could change so rapidly in Michigan.

"Ellene," Caitlin cried.

Her cry caught Connor's attention, and he saw Ellene waiting at the bottom of the steps, looking gorgeous in deep-red pants with a dressy top of the same color. When she shifted, the fringe along the hem of her top swayed and captivated him.

"Caitlin," she said, opening her arms.

The child bounded into Ellene's embrace for a giant hug, then stepped back. "We didn't see you in the church. Were you there?"

"I was behind you." She lifted her gaze to Connor. "I was surprised to see you here."

"I overheard that you were coming to your parents' church today, and I felt I owed you an apology."

She scowled. "You owed *me* an apology? I think it's the other way around."

Connor noticed Caitlin's confused look. She was watching them as if she were at a tennis match.

"I hope you can forgive me for leaving without a word. You were in the kitchen, and I had to pick up Caitlin."

"When, Daddy?"

He looked at her curious frown. "The other night when you stayed with Mrs. Whitlock."

"I understand," Ellene said. "I'd been very rude. I'm surprised you stayed for dinner."

He grinned. "How could I pass up your mother's cooking after all those years?"

She gave him a tender look.

"But I didn't know it was your birthday dinner," he said, still feeling uneasy about that. "I'm sorry. I could have at least brought you flowers."

"I enjoyed my mother's chocolates," she said.

Connor shoved his hands into his pockets to hide his nervousness. "Your father said you were going to call me to set up an appointment."

"Yes. Yes, I am." She gazed at him a moment. "Do you want to set it now?"

"No, you can call me."

She nodded. "I will. Tomorrow morning, so we both have our calendars."

"That's fine," he said, miserable listening to their stilted conversation. His gaze drifted to her lips. Three weeks ago, he'd kissed those lips, and they'd kissed him back. Why had it come to this?

She took a step backward. "Then we'll talk tomorrow."

"Yes."

Her gaze drifted to Caitlin, and she knelt beside her and gave her a hug. "I'll see you, too, Caitlin, just like I promised."

"And we can play Old Maid and go for a walk by the water."

She gave Connor a frantic look. "We'll see, okay?"

Caitlin frowned. "Pepper misses you, too."

"I miss Pepper and the quiet of the island. I miss you and Pepper both," she said. Her gaze lifted to Connor's. "All of you." She rose, then backed away with a quick wave.

Connor stood transfixed, watching her stride into the parking lot. Caitlin tugged at his jacket to follow, but he didn't. Once again, he had no idea what had happened today nor what to make out of Ellene's comment.

All of you. Had she really missed him, too?

On Monday morning, Ellene cornered her father in his office. She closed the door and sank into the chair across from him. "Please explain about you and Connor, Dad? I haven't had a chance to talk with you alone. Mother was always around, and I didn't want to start anything."

Her father leaned back in his desk chair and propped his feet on an open desk drawer. "Connor called me about the business. He said he needed someone's opinion. We talked. I offered to help him, and he accepted. My financial contribution was small. I did that to let him know I had faith in the business."

"Did he tell you I said the business was doomed to fail?"

He gave a solemn nod. "He did, and he sounded beaten, Ellene. A man needs respect, if nothing more, and if you do nothing else, never hammer a man into the ground even if you think you're doing him a favor."

She felt her back bristle. "I didn't hammer him to the ground. I gave an honest opinion. I didn't want to see Connor take his life savings and inheritance and throw it away."

Her father dropped his feet to the floor and leaned across the desk. "What made you think he would fail?"

"The store was floundering."

"Was Connor the present owner?"

She flinched at the look in her father's eyes. "No, but —"

"No, he wasn't. That's correct. Did you ask Connor how he could make the business thrive? Did you encourage ideas to make it more buyer-friendly? Did you see weaknesses without asking if he had a solution?"

"Yes, but —"

"There's no buts, Ellene. Connor was once a friend. He was more than a friend since you'd committed to marriage. Even if you did change your mind. Why would a so-called long-time friend not listen, not encourage, not brainstorm? Explain that to me?"

She lowered her head, having no answer except her superior feeling that she knew what a good business was.

"You couldn't compare a sport store to a construction business. It's apples and oranges. Connor has experience in sales. You didn't give him the courtesy of asking."

Her fingers knotted in her lap. "Did he tell you that?"

"Connor would never say anything negative about you. He said he respected your opinion, but he felt strongly about his plan and wanted a second opinion."

"Dad, I —"

"You're prideful, Ellene. I probably made you that way, and that's my fault. You're a wonderful woman, but you want things your way. You don't give people credit for having ideas that might be better than yours. I didn't want to start an argument with you, but I'm disappointed, and since you brought it up, I want you to know that."

"I'm sorry." She felt tears sting her eyes. "I'm making a mess out of so many things."

"Don't tell *me* you're sorry. Tell Connor. He's a good man. He's raising a child alone.

He's taking chances to make a good life for that little girl, and I think a man who'd do anything for his daughter's happiness is more than a gentleman. He's a king among men."

A king among men. Connor was that and more. "I'll talk to him, Daddy. I'm seeing him this weekend at the cottage to go over the plans."

Her father arched an eyebrow.

"I promise. I'll talk with him. I don't know if I can undo the damage, but I'll try."

He rose and walked around his desk, resting his hands on her shoulders. "That's all I can ask. You're a good daughter, Ellene. You just have to grow up a little."

Though she was thirty, she figured her dad was right.

CHAPTER FOURTEEN

Connor stood outside holding the screen door and watching Caitlin dash toward Ellene, her arms open like the wings of a bird. His daughter needed to be freed from her loss, but Ellene had only added to it. He felt resentment, wondering what today would bring.

Plans for the cottage, he knew, but what else? He studied Ellene's face as she approached him with Caitlin's hand in hers. Instead of business attire, she wore dark blue slacks and a red top with the same color trim — two of the garments she'd bought from the shop in town.

Besides her outfit, she looked different in another way — assured, but not barricaded behind the aloof business attitude he'd come to dislike. She appeared relaxed, as if she knew who she was, and she liked herself.

She carried her briefcase and a long tube under her arm — the plans, he figured.

He'd been anxious to turn the cottage into a home, but since Ellene had left, the warm feelings he'd had for the cottage had vanished. He felt isolated.

"Hi," he said, walking toward her.

She smiled, a warm smile that held a message he was afraid to decipher. Since they'd been reunited, Ellene had jumped from one attitude to another. He suspected she wanted to rekindle their past relationship but feared the outcome. But why?

Connor longed for times to be the way they'd been before their breakup — so natural — a love so pure and innocent that he could only wince at the impossibility of it now. Too much had happened, too many ruts in life's road, too many dreams shattered.

"I have your plans." She raised the tube like a victory cheer.

"I can't wait to see them," he said, managing a smile, yet feeling on guard, waiting for the moment her business persona would take over.

Caitlin tugged at her arm. "Let's go for a walk by the lake. You can see the ducks."

Ellene caressed the child's head. "I'd love to see the ducks, but your daddy and I —"

"We have work to do," Connor said.

Caitlin scrunched her face and kicked at a stone.

Her behavior upset him, and he bent to her level and tilted her chin upward. "What did I tell you, Cait?"

She gave him an I-don't-want-to-hear-this-again look, then lowered her eyes. "Okay," she muttered.

He rose, disappointed in her attitude.

"Here's an idea," Ellene said. "After we look at the plans and talk a while, then we'll go for a walk, okay?"

"Okay," Caitlin said, an accepting look growing on her face.

Connor beckoned to Ellene and headed for the screen door.

"Daddy?"

He halted and faced Caitlin again.

She eyed him a moment as if testing the water. "Can I go play with Pepper for a while?"

A sigh escaped him. "If Aunt Phyllis doesn't mind."

"I'll ask her," she said, pivoting on her heel and skipping across the lawn.

"She's back to her old ways," Connor said, watching her vanish around the corner.

"You've spoiled her, I'm afraid. I know someone else like that, and it causes nothing but problems."

She caught him by surprise, and he studied her face to see if he'd understood what she meant. "She is spoiled, I know. I've tried to please her every whim since Melissa died, and now it's out of hand. She thinks the world revolves around her."

"*Your* world does."

He studied her a moment, realizing she was right.

She gave him a wan smile.

"I suppose that's the problem," he said.

"You can do a lot of things for her — protect her, support her, love her — but you can't spoil her. That's not doing her a favor, nor yourself. Discipline has to be firm but loving. I know. My dad's learning that, too."

This time Connor kicked at a stone, uncomfortable with her message. "You're talking about yourself, I'm guessing."

"I am." She held up the blueprint. "But that's another issue. Do you want to see these first?"

He preferred to talk first, curious as to what she had on her mind, but she looked so excited about the architect's plans. "Let's go."

He pushed open the screen door and held it while Ellene walked inside. She headed for the dining-room table and dropped her case, then pulled the blueprint from the tube and spread it on the table. She waited a moment while he studied the print.

"What do you think?" She gestured to the floor plan.

He could tell she was pleased with the drawing, and he only wished he could concentrate on it and not on the unsaid things that raced through his mind.

He pulled out a chair and sat, gazing at the plan and trying to envision the rooms.

She pointed to the second-floor plan. "See, Caitlin's room is larger. Here's the closet space and bathroom, plus a large walk-in closet here for linens and storage."

"I like that." He shifted his focus to the other renovation — the new front room and screened porch.

She pointed to the details. "It's like a sun-room with wide windows so you can look out to the channel, and there's the window opening. It will have a wide ledge so you can pass dishes outside to the screened porch."

"It's nice," he said, realizing he'd missed something important.

"You sound disappointed."

"No. I like what I see here, but I just thought about the situation when the ferry service was closed. The cottage will still have only two bedrooms. And the downstairs bathroom is so small."

She grinned. "I'm glad you agree."

"Agree?" He saw a playful look on her face.

"What do you think about this?" She pulled another floor plan from beneath the original. Connor saw the dramatic change. She'd added a wing off the bath-and-bedroom hallway, adding another room and expanding the bathroom. "You thought of it all," he said, admiring the plans, yet thinking of the added financing needed.

"I read your mind," she said. "When I stayed here, I knew you were disturbed by the lack of sleeping space, and I wanted to surprise you. There's even a large storage closet on this floor." She pointed to the area. "I know it's an added expense, but you'll be surprised. This part won't have a second floor so it'll be less expensive than you might think."

He looked into her eyes and knew it was time to talk. "Have a seat," he said, motioning toward a chair.

She shifted the chair and sat near him.

"First, I'm really pleased with your work. When I told your dad I trusted your opinion, I meant that. You know my likes and my lifestyle." He gave a wry smile. "All right, you *knew* them, but I still think you know me well enough to know my mind as you did with the addition." He laid the estimates on the table.

"I'm glad you like it, Connor. It's difficult working for a friend. It can cause problems."

"No problems on this," he said, pleased she'd admitted he was a friend, yet sensing she had more to say.

"Do you want to talk while we have a little privacy? Caitlin will be gone a while, I think, and I sense you have something on your mind."

Her expression changed, and he noticed her discomfort.

"I do, Connor. I don't even know where to begin. The problem is mine. So I'll just ramble on and hope it makes sense to you."

She began, and Connor listened. He'd heard much of it before, but this time he sensed something new and more profound.

Ellene seemed to relax after she'd talked for a while. "I told a friend of mine that the lamp of the soul is the eyes, and when I look into your eyes, I can see your soul. You're so honest, Connor. You shared so much with me. You trusted me, and I let you down."

Her comment punched him like a boxer's glove. He had told her most, but not everything, and if they were ever to make progress in their relationship, he needed to be totally honest. But each time they seemed to reach an understanding, something happened to send her off the deep end, and he feared if he told her the truth, it would happen again.

He lowered his head. "Let's not go there, Ellene. It's enough we're making sense now."

"No, I have to. My father reminded me of some things that I have to face. For one, I'm spoiled. I wanted the world to revolve around me, just like you said Caitlin thinks the world revolves around her. I was the center of my parents' lives. My parents gave me everything I wanted, but it took me too long to learn that the real world doesn't work that way."

"Habits are hard to break."

"They are, and I'm not perfect."

"Really?" he said, sending her a teasing grin.

She ignored his humor. "But I hope I've grown a little. At least now I'm aware of it. In the past days, I've been looking back over the things I did to you, Connor — not just in the past, but recently. I showed you no respect, and it wasn't because I don't respect you, but to please my own ego."

"If this is an apology, I accept it."

"It's more than an apology. God sees pride as a sin. I need to be forgiven — by you, God and myself."

"You can count on at least two out of the three, Ellene. When you're humble — and you have been — God honors you and forgives you. You know you have my forgiveness, but I can't help you forgive yourself. You have to do that alone."

She ran her palm along his arm, and her touch sparked his senses. "I'm working on that. And I realized something else. I've spent a lifetime waiting for you to apologize to me, and you have nothing to apologize for. You reacted as anyone would who'd been rebuffed by a fiancée. I hurt you to the core."

"I could have tried harder."

"You did, Connor. You called, and I wouldn't talk. I played games with our relationship, just as you said, and you know what? I'm guessing our marriage would have failed. I wasn't mature enough."

Her words prickled down his arms. "What about now?"

Her eyes met his. "I hope I'm maturing, but only time will tell. I can give you this promise. What I've said is from my heart."

Ellene's gaze captured his, and he read so much in her eyes. He saw her move closer, and his pulse raced when she leaned across the table and cupped his jaw. Her mouth drew nearer, and he felt her lips caress his.

As naturally as sunshine, he laid his palm against her cheek, his other hand exploring the tendrils of her hair.

She eased her lips away, her words playing on his mouth. "That's my promise," she murmured. "I'm not playing lightly with your heart. I want us to learn to trust each other. For now, I'd love you to be my dearest friend."

Connor wanted to be more than dearest friends, but that was a start. He leaned forward, brushing another kiss on her lips. "The dearest," he agreed, hoping she understood. He kissed her again, then stood and drew her beside him. "Let's get Caitlin. She's been so anxious to spend time with you."

"And so have I with her," she said.

He wrapped his arm around her shoulders as they headed out the door.

Connor studied Ellene's face as she sat in his St. Clair Shores living room, amazed that three weeks had passed since their talk on the island. His confidence in their relationship had grown, and each day he shook his head, grateful that Ellene had been open with her feelings that day.

"I can't believe how fast that crew is working. They've already —" Hearing a noise, Connor stopped in mid sentence. He rose from his chair and walked to the doorway leading to the kitchen. "They've already parked a huge Dumpster alongside the house at the cottage," he continued, heading back into the room, "and the crew has torn down the partition between the upstairs rooms. It's a big space."

"I'm anxious to see it." With a curious look, she glanced toward the doorway. "Hearing things?"

"I thought I heard the back door," he said. "Caitlin should be home from school. Sometimes the knob doesn't turn."

"Soon you won't have to worry about that doorknob."

"I know. It'll be so nice to get into the new house with everything working right."

"How's Caitlin handling the move? She seemed fine when I talked with her the other day."

"She's okay with everything when you're around. You're like a salve that makes things better."

"It can't be me."

Connor shook his head. "Don't kid yourself. Caitlin's still moody. I've hoped she would get excited. Maybe she will when she sees what they're doing to her room."

Ellene brushed a strand of hair from her cheek. "I'm sure she will. She'll love it."

"I've asked her to start packing up some of her things so we can get them moved over to the cottage. A few things each trip will make it easier when the time comes. We have to be out of here in another week."

"I can help, Connor. Tell me what to do."

"You've already helped. I appreciate everything. Getting that crew out to the island so quickly shocked me. I figured it would take until midsummer before they even got started."

She grinned. "Not when the job's a priority."

"You did that for me?"

A wry smile lit her face. "No, Daddy did. He's your fan."

"And my partner."

She shifted in the chair. "I know. That really upset me when I heard it. I blamed you — a kind of get-even vendetta, I thought — but I talked with my —"

"Ellene, I'm not the vendetta type. I've made lots of mistakes, but I've never hurt you on purpose."

Her eyes flashed, and he guessed her thoughts.

"The problem with my marriage to Melissa was my fault. I didn't use good sense. My sense of self-worth was nil. I hadn't planned to hurt anyone. I still loved —"

She held up her hand to stop him. "I know. It's the trust factor. I've had some problems with trust, but let's get back to the partnership. I'm okay with it now." She leaned forward. "So, how is the business?"

"Okay," he said, unwinding his thoughts and forcing himself to answer her question. "It still needs work, but I think customers are noticing the difference. Tomorrow's Saturday. How about coming to the island in the afternoon? You can see the cottage and I'll show you around the store."

A scowl settled on her face. "Are you sure you want me to? I seem to put my foot in my mouth."

"I want you to, and let me allay your fears. I'm not going to be like Mr. Long, if that's what you're worrying about. I put a lot of hours and energy into this business, and it's difficult with Caitlin. You know that."

"I'm sorry, Connor." She fell against the chair back and shook her head. "I wasn't trying to be smart with you. I only wondered —"

"Forget it."

An uneasy expression settled on her face.

"Okay, but I want you to know I'm trying to change."

He looked discouraged. "Maybe it's me, but I hear something in your voice. It's a tone."

"What tone?"

"It's just something in the sound of your voice."

"I sound prideful . . . self-important?" Her question rang with discouragement. "If so, I'm trying to do better, Connor."

"It's just a tone. And thanks for realizing it bothers me."

Ellene rose, and when she reached his side, she sat on the chair arm and wrapped her arm around his back. "Connor, I need so much work. I wish I could hire a crew to renovate me. That would be so much easier. And keep being honest, okay?"

Honest. The word struck him. "Nothing in this world is easy, and while we're talking honesty —" He fumbled. "I need to clear the air. I've been avoiding something I need to tell you."

A scowl raced to her face. "Avoiding what?"

He scooted over and slid her onto his lap. "We've come far in the past couple of weeks, and I hope you can understand —"

"Tell me," she said, squirming sideways to look into his face. "What's this about?"

"Daddy!" Caitlin's voice cut through her question.

Ellene gave a start as Connor jumped upward, dumping her into the chair. She felt as if he'd taken her to the brink of a chasm and then hung her over the edge. What about his past? What hadn't he told her that would be that important? Her mind flew with speculation. She had to know.

"Connor?"

He turned, his face drained. "Later," he said, rising to greet Caitlin.

His daughter gave him a cursory hug, then focused on Ellene. "I thought it was you," she said, grinning as she bounded across the carpet toward her.

"How was school?" Ellene asked, managing to keep her voice steady.

"Good."

Caitlin hoisted herself onto Ellene's lap and fondled the collar on her blouse.

"I like the flowers," she said, touching each of the blossoms on the fabric.

Ellene wanted to scream, not at the child, but at the bad timing.

Later? When would later be? She couldn't stay late. She had errands to run, and she knew Caitlin wouldn't leave her side. She pinched the flesh beneath her nose, trying to regain her composure.

"What's wrong?" Caitlin asked, a frown etching her face.

Ellene scrambled for a response. "Nothing. I was just thinking about you."

"I think about you, too. I think about when you were on the island with us. Remember when we went for the sled ride and we tipped over, and when you went shopping and bought me a sweatshirt and one for you so we could be twins? We had fun."

Ellene looked at the child, thinking that life just wasn't always that fun. "I remember."

"Caitlin," Connor said, "change your school clothes so you don't get them dirty."

"Daddy," she whined. "I always have to do things."

Ellene looked away, agreeing with Caitlin, but that was being an adult. "Are you packed and ready to move?"

"We're not moving yet."

"But soon, your dad said."

"I know, but I don't know what to pack."

Ellene rubbed her arm, realizing Connor wasn't going to say a word with Caitlin nearby. "Would you like me to help you for a while? I can't stay long though."

Caitlin's face brightened "Okay," she said, slipping off Ellene's lap. She turned to Connor. "Where are the boxes?"

"I set two in your room. I told you."

"I forgot." She beckoned to Ellene, then headed for her bedroom.

Ellene rose, giving Connor a questioning look.

"Are you coming?" Caitlin called from the doorway.

Connor gave her a helpless look. "Don't worry, Ellene. It's just something I want you to know, but now's not good."

Ellene knew he wouldn't budge. "I'll call you later then."

"This isn't a phone conversation. Please. Maybe tomorrow."

"Tomorrow? You mean at the cottage."

He shrugged. "Yes, if we can find a minute alone."

"Ellene!" Caitlin called.

"Coming," she said.

CHAPTER FIFTEEN

Ellene stood just inside Caitlin's doorway and looked at the pile of toys filling the walls, bookshelves loaded with books and clothes strewn around the room.

"Pretty messy," Ellene said, giving her a chastening grin.

Caitlin sank to the floor, flipping one of her tops with her feet. "I know."

"Where are the boxes?" Ellene gazed around the room and saw two sitting in the corner, draped with a pair of rosy-colored cords. She tugged at the boxes, then dragged them to the middle of the room.

Caitlin fidgeted beside the boxes, dragging clothing toward her with her feet.

"I thought you wanted me to help you," Ellene reminded the child.

"I do," she whined.

"You said *help.* That means we both work, not just me. And you know what? It has to be done, so once you get it finished, it's not a problem anymore. You'll have time to play with no one nagging you."

Caitlin thought that over and raised to her knees. "But I don't know what to do."

Ellene sat on the edge of the unmade bed. "First, let's put your clothes away, or if they're dirty, pile them by the door."

Caitlin didn't move at first, and Ellene began to understand Connor's discouragement. Ellene didn't budge, either, but glanced at her watch. "Too bad. Time's flying, and I have to leave soon."

Finally, Caitlin got to her feet and picked up the clothing she'd been fiddling with. She dropped it by the door, then gathered some other items.

Ellene rose and handed her hangers as she worked at disposing of the garments. "Now, what toys can you live without for a week? Those are the ones you should pack. Leave a few things you'd like to have here."

"I like it when you're here," Caitlin said, as she dropped toys into the carton.

"Thank you. I like being with you."

Caitlin held a toy suspended in her hand. "I don't remember my mommy very well anymore."

"I'm sorry about that, Cait."

"I have a picture." She shifted things on her dresser and carried back a framed photo of a young woman with fleshy cheeks and short brown hair. She had the same shape nose as Caitlin and a similar smile.

Ellene's chest tightened watching the child study at her mother's image. "Your mom's pretty. I can see you in her smile."

"You can?" Caitlin drew the photograph closer so that her nose nearly pressed on the glass.

"Aunt Phyllis says I look like my daddy."

Caitlin lowered the photograph and looked at her as if asking what she thought.

"Your eyes. They're just like your daddy's. They're beautiful."

Ellene saw her tilt her head toward the mirror over her short dresser. She grimaced and smiled, trying on different faces until Ellene laughed. "You look like a monkey when you make all those faces." Ellene stood behind her and rested her hands on her shoulders.

Caitlin's gaze raised from the mirror to Ellene's face. "You're beautiful, too."

"Thank you."

She turned to face Ellene and wrapped her arms around her waist. "I wish you were my mommy now."

Ellene's heart plummeted to her stomach and bounced back. "I know it's difficult not having a mother, Caitlin. Your daddy tries to be a mother and father to you."

"I love my daddy," Caitlin said, "but I want you to be my mommy."

Ellene's heart ached for the child. Her pulse skipped, trying to find a response that the girl could understand. "I'd be honored to be your mother, Caitlin, but being your mom means that your daddy and I would have to fall in love and get married."

"Okay."

Caitlin's matter-of-fact response made Ellene grin. She lifted her gaze and saw Connor standing outside the door. He gave her an uneasy look, then moved away from the door.

"Daddy said if I pray, God will hear my prayers. So I'll pray that you and daddy —"

Ellene knelt in front of the child. "Caitlin, we can pray for things, but God doesn't always say yes. I really like your daddy a lot, but that's something only your daddy and I can decide."

"You, Daddy and God," Caitlin said, her voice ringing with confidence.

And God. The child's words hit her with awareness. Ellene had done much soul-searching, but she hadn't put her problem in God's hands and it was time she did.

She drew the girl into her arms and held

her. Her thin body molded against Ellene's, and Caitlin's fragrance of grape juice and apples filled her senses. She loved the girl more than she could say. Life would never be the same without Caitlin and Connor, and yet he had a secret to tell her, something he'd avoided.

Her nerves felt raw having had Connor let the conversation drop in the middle of something so important. She wanted to know what it was, but not today. Maybe tomorrow, she hoped.

She had her own confession, and it had been on her mind for so long. Sometimes she wondered if Connor would just laugh and say it was nothing. Other times she feared he would be so disappointed it would destroy their relationship. She'd even considered not saying anything at all, but one thing she'd been taught from childhood, honesty was next to godliness in her parents' eyes.

God had the answer, but Ellene wanted it, too. She needed God's help, and she needed patience.

"What do you think?" Connor asked, while Ellene surveyed the construction work in the upstairs bedroom area.

"It's much bigger than it looked on paper."

"I told you that." Connor chuckled.

She gave him a wry smile.

"This is my room," Caitlin said, sticking to Ellene's side. "My toys are downstairs, though, because the work guys would fall over the boxes. That's what Daddy said."

"And he's right." Ellene tousled her hair. "It's a really nice room, though."

"I know and it's bigger than my room in St. Clair Shores."

"I know," Ellene said, letting Caitlin pull her away while she explained what the room would look like when it was finished.

Connor saw the look on Ellene's face, and he knew she was thinking about their interrupted conversation. He feared she'd blown the content out of proportion. Before they could finish the talk, he had to find something to preoccupy Caitlin.

If he and Ellene were to make a go of their relationship, everything had to be on the table — everything out in the open, no secrets. Marriages were difficult enough without either partner hiding something significant from his or her past.

Maybe he wanted to tell Ellene as much for himself as for her. He'd felt guilty throughout his marriage to Melissa and worse after she died. He'd remained true to her, but the devotion he'd wanted to feel hadn't been there.

"This will be a mess to live in for a while," Ellene said, stepping over a stack of two-by-fours, then dodging a pile of drywall. "At least the insulation is up. They should get to the walls on Monday."

"They said it could be ready to paint next weekend."

Aunt Phyllis's voice sailed up the staircase. "Are you upstairs?"

"We're here," Connor said, turning to make his way down to the first floor. Ellene and Caitlin followed.

When they reached the bottom, his aunt opened her arms to Ellene. "I thought that was your car in the driveway." She hugged Ellene, then stepped back. "Have you been to the store yet?"

"No, we're going in a few minutes. Would you like to come along."

"Thanks, but no. I just wanted to say hello. And a verse came to mind on my way over."

Connor felt his back stiffen. "A verse?"

"From Job," his aunt said.

"Job. Now that sounds ominous."

"Job was a man of faith who suffered

many trials but continued to love the Lord, Connor."

He nodded his head like a head-bobbing doll until he stopped himself. "I know about Job, Aunt Phyllis. So what's the verse?"

She arched an eyebrow. "The verse is for Ellene. 'Your beginnings will seem humble, so prosperous will your future be.' "

Ellene seemed to study his aunt's face, as if trying to figure out what the scripture meant to her. "Thank you," she said.

From her expression, Connor assumed she didn't know what the verse meant, but he had a guess. He shifted his attention to Caitlin, praying she'd agree. "Do you want to stay with Aunt Phyllis? We'll only be gone a short time."

"I want to —" She began in a whiny voice, then stopped as if remembering. "I want to go with you and Ellene," she said in a pleasant tone.

"You asked very nicely, Caitlin," he said, giving Ellene a quick look to explain why he couldn't say no. "You can come along, too." He sent up a quick prayer that God would help him find some time during her visit to have their talk.

"Goodie," she said, giving him a smile.

Ellene gave him a private shrug as if she understood he had no choice, and they ambled to the car with Aunt Phyllis chattering as if she'd never see them again.

"We'll only be gone an hour or so," he said. "We'll see you when we get back."

"That's fine, but remember the verse, Ellene." She patted her arm as she passed and headed toward her house.

Pepper's bark sounded at the open windows, and Connor could hear his aunt shushing the dog as they climbed into the car.

Once inside, Ellene frowned as she clamped her seatbelt. "Did that verse make sense to you?"

"You know my aunt," he said, checking behind him to see that Caitlin was buckled in. He turned back, avoiding a direct answer, because he didn't want to presume anything, but he figured it was his aunt's way of tempering Ellene's attitude.

As they headed toward town, Connor viewed the landscape — the blossoming wildflowers along the road's edge, the budding trees, the tulips and daffodils sprouting from residents' flower beds. Spring had finally come, and with it a warm breeze that blew off the lake.

"The air smells so fresh," Ellene said as the wind billowed through the half-open window. "The island looks so pretty this time of year."

"The circle of life, things die and are reborn in spring." His own circle of life hung in his mind.

"That's in the *Lion King,* Daddy," Caitlin said, then began singing in her piping voice, getting most of the words wrong.

"Sing, Ellene," she called, trying to lean over the seat, though the seatbelt held her back.

"I'd rather listen to you," Ellene said, glancing over her shoulder.

Caitlin continued to sing. Sometimes the songs were tuneless — ones she made up, Connor figured — but other times he recognized the tune.

Connor's emotions throbbed, knowing that today he would tell Ellene everything, yet he was touched, too, seeing the two women who meant so much to him chattering together in the most natural way.

Sometimes he questioned his sanity. Why had he pursued Ellene for so long? Why had she stayed in his heart? He wasn't sure he believed that each person had a soul mate, but for some reason, he'd often sensed that he and Ellene were meant to be together. As his faith grew, he attributed the feeling to part of God's divine plan. Other times he wondered if the feeling was his own will and had nothing to do with God.

"How do Christians know for sure their choices are God's will?" He heard himself ask the question aloud, and it startled him.

Ellene snapped to attention. "That's a strange question."

Caitlin's song faded. "Daddy, that's a strange question," she mimicked.

"It just popped into my head," he said to both of them.

"We have to pray and ask God to assure us," Ellene said. "It can be a gut feeling that this is right and good."

"I don't always trust my gut feelings."

"I know, but sometimes things happen that make it so easy to know. Let's say you wanted to go someplace, but you didn't have the money, and then one day you open an envelope and you find a rebate check or a shareholder bonus for the exact amount you needed. That seems as if God is saying, trust me, trust your instincts."

He nodded. "That makes sense, but not everything is that evident."

"No, but you have to do things on faith, too. You ask God to help you decide. When you can't imagine things going in any other direction but the one that sticks in your mind, then you can assume it's God's choice."

He nodded, amazed that God had persisted to bring them together.

As he drove along the main street, Connor saw cars filling many of the parking slots. He felt good, knowing people were out shopping. He had tremendous hopes for his sport store.

He made his way to his private parking place behind the store, turned off the ignition and unhooked his belt. "Here we are."

They spilled from the car and headed into the back of the store, passing through the employees' workroom. He watched Ellene survey the mess with questioning eyes, and when they stepped into the store, her inspection became more intense.

"The shelves are still dusty," she said, dragging her finger across the display shelf and showing him the gray smudge on her finger.

"I'm working hard on building stock," he said, "but while you're here, feel free." He ducked back into the workroom and when he came out, he tossed her a dustcloth.

She eyed it, and he saw her bite her bottom lip while her head swayed back and forth.

He walked closer to her and grasped her shoulders. "It's okay. I'm pleased you're willing to dust."

He spun away, leaving her standing alone with a surprised expression while he enjoyed the teasing. When his eyes shifted, he saw Caitlin trying to climb onto an exercise bike that had just arrived in the store.

"Be careful," he said, hurrying to her side.

"I will." She eyed the pedal too low for her reach. "You should get these for little kids, Daddy."

He chuckled. "Little kids ride real bikes. You don't need a pretend one."

"Yes, I do."

He gave her a wink and glanced over her shoulder at Ellene. She'd taken him at his word, and he watched her a moment while she dusted the shelves near the employees' doorway. "Hey, you," he called, beckoning her forward.

She shifted toward him, still carrying the cloth. "Leave that by the door," he said, "and thanks."

She dropped the cloth by the doorway and came to meet him. "What?"

"Look around."

She finally noticed. "Exercise equipment. Great idea."

"Thanks."

"And I'll have bikes available soon, lots of new products."

She wandered around the front of the

store, looking at new items and evaluating his progress, he was sure, but instead of a frown, she turned with a smile. When she made her way back to where he waited, she opened her arms and gathered him into an embrace. "Really nice, Connor. I see lots of new things."

"And more to come, including a good spring cleaning."

"Your beginnings will seem humble, so prosperous will your future be." She chuckled. "Dear Aunt Phyllis. She certainly has a way with words, doesn't she?"

"But not her words," he said.

"No, God's Word. Talk about the Lord's guidance." She flung out her arms, then let them flop to her sides. "I need to listen to your aunt more carefully."

"I think she has a direct connection to God."

"Daddy," Caitlin said, tugging on his arm.

"What, Cait?"

"I think Aunt Phyllis talks to God a lot 'cuz I hear her mumbling whenever I go over there and no one's there, except Pepper."

He brushed his hand across her soft hair. "And God had better listen to Aunt Phyllis."

"Right," Caitlin said, "Because she's old

and we have to listen to old people."

Connor watched Ellene's grin widen to a smile, and he grinned, too.

"That's why you have to listen to me," he said to Caitlin.

"You're not real old, Daddy. Just a little."

"Thank you, Cait."

"Out of the mouth of babes," Ellene whispered.

CHAPTER SIXTEEN

"Finally," Connor said, leaning against the kitchen counter.

Though he was trying to look relaxed, Ellene saw tension flicker on his jawline. She knew the time had finally come to talk.

She stood by the side door, watching Caitlin jig alongside Aunt Phyllis as they went to her house to make cookies. "She's a good girl, Connor. I know you're proud of her."

"Prouder than I can say. She riles me sometimes, but it's my own frustration."

Ellene turned from the door and crossed to his side. "If you watch any of those talk shows, you'll see the problems aren't only with single parents. All kinds of families struggle with the same problems, and they can last for years. The only thing parents can do is their best — and pray."

Connor lowered his head. "I probably don't pray enough for Caitlin. I just get frustrated. I know she needs so much, and I have so little to give."

"How can you say that?"

He lifted his gaze, his brows raising in question.

"Don't shortchange yourself, Connor. I envy some of your qualities. I wish I had more patience and humility like you do. Do you want a list? You're the epitome of kindness, good humor, compassion, gentleness, morals and honesty. What else is there?"

He pushed himself away from the counter, shaking his head. "And now you've brought us back to yesterday."

"Yesterday?"

A scowl weighted his face. "The thing I need to talk with you about." He beckoned to her. "Let's sit for this."

Let's sit for this. The words sounded ominous, and though she had wanted to know the truth, her pulse rose as she followed him across the great room to the sofa.

He lowered his arms to his thighs and wove his fingers into a tight knot, dangling them between his knees. He looked from her to the floor, then back again. "I want us to have a clean slate, Ellene — everything out in the open."

His pulse escalated as she searched his eyes. "I avoided telling you some things, and

I suppose that makes my avoidance a lie."

A lie. Her heart rose to her throat.

"When I said I didn't want Caitlin a while ago, I'd meant it. I didn't want Caitlin or any child. Melissa's pregnancy was an accident."

She heard herself gasp. "How can you say that? You're her father."

"I love Caitlin with all my heart and soul. I'd never give her back even if God could reverse life and I had a second chance. She is the joy of my heart, but at the time, I felt duped and stupid."

Duped and stupid? Ellene sat dazed.

Connor hung his head. "I've asked God to forgive me, but at the time I wasn't rational. I felt trapped."

Duped, stupid, trapped? "You're upsetting me, Connor. I'm totally bewildered."

"I was bewildered and bitter — mainly at myself. It's a long story, and you know part of it. When you broke off with me, I was angry, and I figured if you were playing games so could I. I went out on a couple of empty dates, then I called you, but you were as defiant as anyone could be. My vendetta was to get even and show you that you weren't the only fish in the sea."

"So you dated and got involved with women. You told me."

"I dated a few women, but I only got involved with one, Melissa. She desired me and I took advantage, but I still had dreams of letting time pass until you realized that I was the man for you."

Ellene's chest tightened until she feared she couldn't breathe. "You were intimate with her. If you still loved me, why did you do that?"

"Anything I say will sound like a weak excuse. When I left you I felt so worthless and empty. I couldn't imagine anyone finding me appealing. Melissa did. She wanted my love, and she seemed open to intimacy. I'd wanted to share that with you, but then it seemed impossible."

Ellene lowered her eyes. "I'd expected you to beg for a while," she whispered, "until you gave me what I wanted — more of your time."

"But you had my heart, Ellene." He pressed his hand against his chest while sadness filled his eyes. "Do you think I didn't find you attractive? I respected you too much to pressure you. I respected your faith. I admired it and wished I felt as strongly as you did about values."

Ellene caught her breath.

"I wasn't raised that way, but you and your family taught me so much. Allowing myself to fall into sinful behavior so soon after our breakup made me feel rotten. You have been so staunch, so moral, and I've loved you for that all these years."

Ellene's heart rose to her throat. He'd given her credit that she didn't deserve. Her indiscretions gnawed at her like a hungry tiger. "Why didn't you ask, Connor? I never understood your need."

Connor jerked away from her and rose. "What need? Need had nothing to do with it. My need was to be loved by you. I just told you I admired your strength. I envied your morals and faith. I didn't *need* anything that would change all that I respected."

"Did you respect your wife?"

Connor sank back into the cushion and covered his face with his hands. She leaned forward, embracing his shoulders. "I'm sorry, Connor. That was a mean question."

"It's a logical question, Ellene." He turned his head to look into her eyes. "I made the best out of it. I was faithful to Melissa, but I never loved her as I should have. I did care about her."

"Then why did you marry her?"

He drew back, his face pale. "I told you I married her on the rebound, but that's been my biggest lie."

Ellene's stomach twisted while her mind raced for an answer, but nothing made sense. "Tell me why?"

"I didn't use protection. She told me she'd taken care of it, but she hadn't."

"She got pregnant?"

He nodded.

"You married her because she was pregnant?"

"I'd let my morals slip, but I knew what was right. We got married, and that's why the wedding was so sudden. She was the mother of my child. What could I do?"

Ellene remembered counting the months on her fingers, trying to understand when they'd broken up and when Caitlin was born, but the brief thought had slipped from her mind.

"I should have told you about this from the beginning. Can you forgive me?" he asked.

Ellene's head spun. "You're already forgiven. I need to forgive myself."

He shifted closer and captured her hands, pressing his lips to her fingers. "We were both at fault. The lies are gone. I feel as if a weight has lifted from my shoulders."

She looked into his face, seeing his jaw relax, the concern in his eyes gone. "I'm so sad about this, Connor, but never say you wish you hadn't married Melissa. If you hadn't, Caitlin wouldn't be part of our lives. She's so like you. Thank God for her."

Connor placed his thumb beneath her chin and tilted her head upward. "Thank you for understanding and for reminding me of the blessing."

His gaze clung to hers as his mouth lowered to a kiss. She languished in the sweet sensation that felt so perfect and so right.

Connor drew back, his nose touching hers, his lips brushing hers as he spoke. "I can't tell you how you've made things so complete and full for us, and you love Caitlin, which is all I could ever ask."

He straightened his back, his hands grasping hers again. "Do you think we could start over? Do you think we could make it work now? We've resolved everything, forgiven everything."

Ellene's heart thundered. But they hadn't. He'd called her morally strong, and she had to tell him the truth about her own actions. His openness only made her weakness more excruciating.

"Yesterday, at my house, I overheard Caitlin. I think you saw me." He squeezed her hand, studying her face.

She nodded, letting him know she had seen him.

"She said she wanted you to be her mommy."

"I know. She startled me." She looked away, his gaze too intense.

He drew her face around to his. "I want the same thing, Ellene. Will you marry me? Will you be my wife and Caitlin's mommy?"

The floor fell out from under her. The proposal was all she'd ever dreamed and all she'd ever hoped, but not now, not until —

"I need time, Connor."

His eyes widened, bewilderment glinting in their depth. "Time? What have we been doing? We've had years, and now I thought we'd grown. I sense you care about me."

"I do, Connor, but we don't want to make a mistake."

"A mistake? You're kidding. How could this be a mistake? God's led us back together. I feel it in my gut."

"If God brought us together, then a couple of days, a week won't make any difference."

He drew himself upward up, shaking his head. "Not again. I can't take this anymore, Ellene. I really can't."

"Connor, please. I —"

Dismay filled his face. He rose and

charged across the room, grasping the kitchen counter before he swung back. "I give up."

Panic rushed over her. She'd been about to make the same mistake she'd made so often. Cowardice. She didn't have time to think how to tell him. Lord, give me the words. "Connor, please." She patted the sofa. "Please, sit for a minute. I need to tell you something."

He didn't move but clung to the kitchen counter, rocking on his heels, his gaze away from her. Finally he turned and his look broke her heart.

He plodded across the room and dropped onto the sofa while his gaze probed hers.

A ragged breath tore from her chest. It should be nothing after all this time — an indiscretion — but she knew better. She'd spent her life disappointed in herself and ashamed at what she'd done. Her action hadn't been what the Lord expected. And to add to her shame, Owen had walked away, too, leaving her feeling unclean.

Connor's brow furrowed and his mouth looked pinched. "You have to tell me what?" He looked at her, a frown growing on his face. "You know, I think I've heard every excuse and every reason for what's gone wrong with our relationship. I take part of the blame. I was ashamed to tell you about Melissa's pregnancy, afraid you'd be disappointed and worse that I would disgust you, but —"

"This has nothing to do with you, Connor. It's my shame, and like you, I've never told you this. You know I dated after we broke up, but I never told you that I made the same mistake as you, Connor."

"You were pregnant?" His mouth dropped open and he seemed paralyzed.

"No, not pregnant, but I've been with a man. I'm not a virgin."

"You're not?" His eyes widened, and a look of disappointment swept over him.

"I'm sorry. I know you're startled. I fell in love, and I took a horrible step outside my faith. I knew you'd be disappointed so I didn't want to tell you."

He lowered his face to his hands. "I wish you'd told me earlier. But how could you sit there for so long without telling me? I've felt guilty for so long, Ellene. I didn't want to hurt you, because I had such admiration for your Christian strength." He lifted his gaze. "I explained this to you, and yet you didn't help me feel better by telling me the truth. I would have understood."

"Connor, I was afraid, too, afraid I'd disappoint you."

"I am disappointed. I'm disappointed in your lack of trust that I wouldn't understand."

"I told you a while ago that I had a trust issue. You know I've had a difficult time trusting you, and Owen, the guy I was almost engaged to, left me after promising me the moon. How could I trust any man?"

"Because you knew me. You *know* me. You know my child and my likes and dislikes. How can we have a marriage without trust? I'm sorry, but this time I need time to think."

He shifted away from her, grabbing the doorknob. He swung the door open and vanished outside.

Ellene sat alone and miserable.

Connor rounded the corner of the house and headed down to the channel. He kicked stones as he walked, realizing he lacked trust, too. He bent to select a flat stone and skipped it across the water. It hopped twice, leaving concentric rings as evidence of its passing before it sank into Lake St. Clair. He envisioned his marriage proposal — two proposals — plunging into dark depths, leaving not neat perfect circles but billowing chaos. They'd both been so wrong.

Still, he loved Ellene. What more could he say?

Connor walked with his hands knitted behind his back, watching the seagulls soar and dip above the green water. He'd never been free. He'd been bound by his mistakes and his secret love for Ellene that he'd guarded and refused to let surface for so long.

A groan tore from his throat. Neither had trusted the other enough to be totally honest, and he knew marriage could survive only with complete honesty and trust.

He turned and walked backward, his gaze traveling to his aunt's house where Caitlin was making cookies. Cookies. Such a simple delight to a child. And love. Shouldn't that be a simple delight when it was in God's care?

Foolish that he would even think love could be simple. It was one of the most complex emotions he'd ever felt, but one that filled him to the brim with joy. Caitlin's love made him who he was, a father, a man who wanted the best for his child, a man who loved his country and his God.

Ellene. He loved her with all his heart.

He'd heard a Bible verse once, probably from his aunt, that said God's eyes and heart would always be with His children.

He felt that way about Ellene. She'd been in his eyes and heart forever, it seemed.

He'd reacted badly. He'd made bad choices and so had Ellene. She had a will of her own. God gave His children choices, and sometimes they made grave mistakes. He had, but today they'd both been open and honest. Today was a new beginning.

He crouched in the sand and ran his finger through the grains, making circles like the skipping stones. He could turn chaos into circles. It only took forgiveness and love to smooth the rough places.

A breeze ruffled his hair, and he pulled his fingers through the strands to smooth it. Smooth the rough places. That's what he had to do. His pulse skipped as he organized his thoughts.

"Connor."

He looked up into Ellene's eyes.

"I love you," she said. "I want to marry you and be Caitlin's mommy. I can't imagine life without either of you in it. Having you walk out the door made me realize how you must have felt so long ago." She touched his shoulder with the tips of her fingers.

Connor rose, standing beside her, seeing her chest rise and fall as if she couldn't catch her breath. She'd taken a step. She'd trusted that he loved her, and she'd been right.

He looked into her eyes, feeling his heart swell, his dreams blossoming like the budding trees. "Are you sure?"

"I've never been more sure."

He studied her lovely face, the depth of her eyes, the flush of her cheek, her shiny, dark hair that beguiled him. He lifted his finger and drew it across her jaw to her cheek. He traced the line of her mouth, the soft lips that kissed so sweetly.

Her eyes asked, and his lips answered. They brushed hers, capturing her mouth beneath his, her breath mingled with his, her heart beating against his chest.

She nestled against him and he clutched her like a man clinging to a buoy in a storm, fearing if he let go he would drown.

"I love you," he whispered into her hair. "I accept your proposal."

He heard her chuckle against his cheek. "You proposed to me," she said.

Connor drew back and shook his head. "I asked you inside. You said you needed time. Out here in front of God and nature, you asked me, and I accept."

She captured his hand and kissed his fingers. "Should we go and tell Caitlin?"

"We don't have to. She's been praying and

she believes God answers her prayers."

"So do I," Ellene said.

He drew her back into his arms. "Then we are like-minded, Ellene Bordini."

Her mouth caught his, and it took his breath away.

CHAPTER SEVENTEEN

Three Months Later

Ellene turned one way then another. She didn't know whose call to answer. "What, Aunt Teresa?"

"Where do you keep the large platters?"

"In the high cabinet, or if not, in the new storage room in the hallway. I can't remember where we put them."

She dashed out the side door to answer her Uncle Gino's call.

"There she is," he said, opening his arms.

She moved into his embrace, feeling so loved on this special day.

"Bella, bella," he said, drawing her back and looking into her face. "You're flushing like a true bride. I'm so happy for you."

"Thanks, Uncle Gino.

"And I made you six sheets of focaccia. Nothing's too good for my niece."

"Thanks. We all love your flat bread." She waited for him to tell her why he'd called, and when he didn't, she finally asked. "What did you want?"

"Want?" He gave her a dazed look.

"Oh," he said, chuckling. "How do you want us to set up the chairs? Tito's unloading them from the truck."

She glanced toward the road and saw her cousin piling white folding chairs against a rented van. She grinned, grateful for her faithful family. "Did you see the trellis in the back? We'll be married in front of that. So line them up in rows facing it."

"You got it," he said, his eyes scanning the yard. "Where's the groom?"

"Home." She caught herself. "With his parents. He'll be here in a while, then I have to hide at his aunt's house. Remember, the bride and groom can't see each other on their wedding day until the ceremony."

"Ellene!"

She turned toward the door and saw her mother's arms flapping at her. She shook her head, hoping it was her mother's drama and not a real problem.

"What's up, Mom?" she asked, hurrying toward the door.

"Jimmy's here with the dishes. Do you want them in the new sunroom?"

"Yes. Connor put the huge table there. It'll hold a lot."

She followed her mother to admire the renovated porch that now provided wonderful space with windows and a great view. Standing a moment to catch her breath, Ellene thought back to the first day she'd come to the cottage to talk with Connor about the renovations. It seemed so long ago and yet it was less than five months.

Her heart burst with pleasure, realizing that today she and Connor would be married. They'd planned their dream wedding, the family and a few friends together on the island where they'd rekindled their love — a love Connor had convinced her was directed by God.

Through the window she could see the trellis, and Uncle Gino lining chairs facing the water and the place she and Connor would stand.

When she stepped back into the great room, the scent of pasta sauce and roasting chicken filled the room. Her aunts and cousins darted from cabinet to stove to table, preparing for the wedding reception.

She eyed the dining-room table covered in alacy cloth and piled with trays of Italian cookies — pizzelle, powdered sugar bow ties, miniature cannoli — and in the center of the table, the most beautiful cherry-nut wedding cake from Sweetheart Bakery, decorated with edible orchids. Everything was perfect, and she knew Connor would be so pleased.

Connor. Her pulse skipped with anticipation. How long had it taken for two bull-headed people — and one who was also self-centered — to hear God's voice and follow His leading? And Caitlin. Her heart swelled with joy, calling the child her own.

Ellene headed for the side door. From inside, she could see her relatives raising a white tent. Beneath its shade they would place the long tables for their meal. She stepped outside, knowing that soon the house and grounds would be filled with noisy family that were so precious to her.

"Where do you want them?"

Ellene spun around to see her aunt Carmela coming down the driveway carrying a box. "What are they?"

"The bonbonniere."

"The what?" She strained her neck to see if she could see inside the box.

Her aunt gave her a look that questioned her sanity. "The confetti."

Ellene grinned. How could she forget the Italian wedding tradition? "Put them somewhere under the tent. We'll find a table or something, and I have a basket and lace tablecloth to hold them."

How many times had she come home from a reception carrying a colorful net enclosing five or seven sugar-coated almonds? An uneven number meant good luck and the coated almonds symbolized the bitter and sweet of a marriage. Since Ellene figured she'd already had enough bitter, she looked forward to years of the sweet part.

She eyed her wrist, aware that time was moving too quickly, then went inside. "Mom, I'm going next door. Connor will be here soon, and he can't see me."

Her mother looked up at the wall clock and let out a yelp. "You'd better get moving." She gave Ellene a hug. "Now don't worry about a thing. We'll have everything ready on time."

Ellene's eyes misted, seeing her mother and aunts working so hard to make her wedding a magnificent event. She brushed away the moisture as she crossed the lawn to Aunt Phyllis's.

Connor slid from his car and waited for Caitlin to unbuckle her seatbelt. She looked so sweet in her white ruffled dress with lace and tiny pink flowers. His heart swelled, knowing that next door, his bride, the woman he'd loved for so long was getting ready for their wedding.

His cousin and family pulled up behind him, and he waited until they'd reached his side. "This is it. You remember the cottage?"

"But it looks different now," Sean said. He turned to his wife. "You should have seen Connor and me when we were kids, Jennifer. We had more fun out here." He lifted his five-year-old son in his arms. "Daddy used to stay overnight here when he was a little boy like you."

"Can I stay over the night?" the boy said.

Sean laughed, and Connor beckoned them up the sidewalk to the tent. "We'll move the chairs up here after the ceremony. If you can help, I'd appreciate it."

"No problem," Sean said, passing Connor with his family to walk toward the channel. "It's a beautiful day and a nice setting for your wedding. The place looks really nice from the outside with the renovations."

And it would be even nicer. "Thanks. Wait until you see inside." Connor took a long look at his new home, a home that would be filled with love, faith and hope. The lonely, guilt-ridden days were over. Ellene had changed his life, and she'd helped Caitlin so much through a difficult time.

"There you are."

Connor turned and waved at Syl, who'd

been as supportive as any father could be, and Connor had been pleased to hand his partner a check to pay back a small part of his backing. The store had been doing well, and Connor was confident the new features had made the difference. He'd felt so thankful when Ellene had pitched in with the pride of an owner. Her hard work had turned the dusty place into a tidy store with a creative front window.

Ellene. His stomach knotted with expectancy. In another twenty minutes, he'd be standing before the pastor, promising to love and honor his wife. That would be easy. He'd loved and honored her for many years.

"Come here," Uncle Gino called, his hands beckoning with wild gyrations.

Connor hurried to him, becoming tangled in a group hug from Ellene's wonderful family. Each gave him words of advice, some laughable, but some that touched his heart. "Never let the sun go down in anger." "Let her know who's boss. She is." The advice was filled with back-pats and guffaws, and he joined in the revelry — an Irishman learning to be Italian. He loved them.

"Hi, Connor."

Connor spun around. "Christine," he said, greeting Ellene's good friend. They'd only met a couple of times, but he liked the woman. She seemed like an older sister to Ellene. "You look great."

"The maid of honor always has to look presentable, and you look dashing." She adjusted his tie.

"Thanks. Have you talked to Ellene?"

"I sure have. She's still there, so I think the wedding's a go."

He laughed, knowing that Christine had been around for all the ups and downs of their relationship.

"It's time, Daddy," Caitlin said, skipping to his side. "The minister said we should all go to the wedding place."

Connor took Caitlin's hand and led the way. At the trellis, he waited, listening to the pastor's simple instructions to Christine and to his cousin Sean, the best man.

The family meandered down the grass and settled into the chairs, their voices resounding over the water. He saw his aunt Phyllis arrive and give a wave to the pastor. She found a chair in the front, then the pastor raised his hands like a blessing. "We will begin," he said.

The family rose and turned to face the side.

Connor's heart stood still when Ellene came into view. Her flowing dark hair hung in tendrils woven with white flowers and ivy. She seemed to float toward him, her silky gown shimmering in the summer light and fluttering in the breeze. The bodice glinted and as she neared, he saw beads shaped like tiny flowers.

His bride. Soon, his wife. Connor's heart overflowed with joy. He lifted his eyes to heaven, whispering a prayer of thanksgiving to the Lord who had blessed him with this wonderful woman. They'd been through so many trials, each second-guessing the other, until they'd nearly destroyed something too wonderful to explain.

"Ellene looks like a princess, doesn't she, Daddy?"

Connor gazed down at Caitlin with tears in his eyes. "She does, Cait, and so do you. You're both the most beautiful women in the world."

"Really?" Her eyes widened, waiting for him to answer.

"Promise," he said.

"That means it's true."

She gave Ellene a tiny wave, and Ellene's face glowed as she gave a small wave back. Syl handed his daughter over to Connor, and they stood hand in hand, listening to the pastor's words, the vows, the exchange of rings, the blessings, but all Connor heard was the beating of his heart and the joy that rang in his ears.

"You may kiss the bride."

Connor heard those words, and with unspeakable joy, he drew Ellene into his arms and kissed her, a kiss that would live in his memory forever.

When they faced the family, the pastor made his final announcement. "I would like to introduce Mr. and Mrs. Connor Faraday."

Her family and friends rose with a cheer, and Ellene squeezed his arm. "I love you, Mr. Faraday."

"And I love you, Mrs. Faraday."

Caitlin shook Connor's arm. "Can I talk?"

"Talk?" He eyed Ellene.

She gave a minute shrug. "Why not?"

"Okay," he said, holding up his hand to the family.

The noise subsided, and he gestured to Caitlin.

She squeezed between them and grinned at Connor, then at Ellene. Finally she turned to the family. "I want you to know that this is my new mommy."

Ellene drew in a breath, then stooped to pull Caitlin into her arms. "And this is my new daughter," she said, "and I love her very much."

The three stood, hand in hand, making

their way to the family, and the noise rose in decibels as women wiped their eyes and men pretended theirs didn't need wiping.

Ellene turned to face Connor and pressed her hand against his cheek. "I've always seen love in your eyes, but I didn't recognize it. Thank you for loving me so long."

Tangled in emotion, Connor couldn't speak, but he knew later he would tell her all the things he kept in his heart, and he would spend the rest of his life showing her how wonderful a blessed love could be.

Dear Reader,

Islands have always interested me. I love the lighthouses and the sense of being in a unique place. I've had the experience of being stranded on Harsens Island, a real place off the base of Michigan's thumb. My adventure lasted only part of a day, but it is true that residents can be stranded for days to weeks.

Sometimes in life, we feel stranded in different ways. We find ourselves feeling lost and not knowing which way to turn. We don't know how to escape. Ellene and Connor were lost in their past, not knowing how to rid themselves of the shame and sadness they felt from acting against God's Word.

When each of us looks into our own lives, I know we can find too many times we have broken commandments or acted against the Lord's wishes. But we have the answer. We know that God has offered us forgiveness through Jesus' death and resurrection if we are truly sorry and if we repent of our sins. Rather than carry the weight of shame and sadness on our shoulders, let us hand them to the Lord who promises to carry the burden for us.

May God bless you and may His light shine on you.

Gail Gaymer Martin

QUESTIONS FOR DISCUSSION

1. Who was your favorite character and why do you relate to this person the most?

2. Ellene wanted to prove to her father she could do a "man's" job. Have you ever been determined to prove to your family or friends that you could accomplish something people thought you couldn't?

3. Ellene held such a strong grudge against Connor, she didn't want to work on the project for him. Have you ever held such a strong grudge against someone, that it affected your behavior?

4. Aunt Phyllis knew her Bible and followed God's will for Christians to be peacemakers. Do you know anyone who uses their gifts to bring peace to dissenting individuals?

5. Though Caitlin loved her daddy, she felt the loss of her mother deeply. Have you known a child who had to deal with a loss? What helped the child?

6. Ellene was stranded on Harsens Island. Have you ever been stranded in a situation that forced you to make the best of a bad situation? Was your attempt successful?

7. Ellene blamed Connor for their breakup, but she finally realizes it usually takes two people to create a problem. Have you ever blamed someone for a problem and then learned you were as much at fault? What did you learn from that?

8. Having intimacy before marriage is too common today. How did this sin affect Ellene's and Connor's lives? How do you deal with this problem as it affects your family and friends?

9. Did you think it was realistic for Connor to be more upset with Ellene's lack of trust than with the secret she told him? Why or why not?

10. What faith message did you learn from this story?

ABOUT THE AUTHOR

Gail Gaymer Martin lives in Michigan with her husband, Bob, her dearest friend and greatest support. She loves the privilege of writing stories that touch people's hearts and share God's promises.

Gail is multipublished in nonfiction and over thirty works of fiction. Her novels have received numerous awards: a Booksellers Best in 2005, a Holt Medallion in 2001 and 2003, the Texas Winter Rose 2003, the American Christian Romance Writers 2002 Book of the Year Award and the *Romantic Times BOOKclub* Reviewers Choice as Best Love Inspired novel in 2002.

When not behind her computer, Gail enjoys a busy life — traveling, presenting workshops at conferences, as well as speaking at churches, business groups and civic events.

She enjoys hearing from her readers. Write

to her at P.O. Box 760063, Lathrup Village, MI, 48076 or at gail@gailmartin.com. Visit her Web site at www.gailmartin.com.

The employees of Thorndike Press hope you have enjoyed this Large Print book. All our Thorndike and Wheeler Large Print titles are designed for easy reading, and all our books are made to last. Other Thorndike Press Large Print books are available at your library, through selected bookstores, or directly from us.

For information about titles, please call:
(800) 223-1244

or visit our Web site at:
www.gale.com/thorndike
www.gale.com/wheeler

To share your comments, please write:
Publisher
Thorndike Press
295 Kennedy Memorial Drive
Waterville, ME 04901